Falcon Strike

By

John L. Hash

Previous works of John L. Hash:

Honey Branches; The Meade Estate

Starkeeper

Lero's Mission

Go Get Nadja

Flight to Oblivion

This book is dedicated to the American Military Contractors, who serve in dangerous areas, provide vital and essential services, and whose sacrifices are many times not noticed on the pages of history.

Chapter 1

The intelligence office where they worked was in a second sub-basement of an older office building.

Each man and woman stationed there carried a special key that would operate the elevator to take them down to the second floor below ground without registering on the signal in the hallway. Twenty eight men and women worked in the office and all communications into the office and from the office were handled by a master cable that ran deeply underground for about two hundred yards until it joined a regular underground utility conduit. All incoming and outgoing data was encrypted, so decoding of the data would be next to impossible even if an enemy espionage effort succeeded in intercepting any of its traffic. Covert operations were not managed out lf this office, but this office monitored coded messages from "projects" and "efforts." Because the agencies and offices that serviced the intelligence efforts of the State of Israel were dispersed throughout Israel, it was felt that better avoidance of detection and interference could be achieved.

A couple of blocks away, the café was hot and crowded. Outside, the noonday throngs of shoppers and shopkeepers and street merchants created quite a din. Inside, though, even without air conditioning, the café was quieter and much cooler. This particular café, on a narrow side street, was having a busy day.

Major Ari Haim and his exec, Captain Tomas Hark were sharing a platter of hummus and having a cup of coffee. They could discuss things quietly here and, with the small table between them, they could speak in hushed tones and catch up on the morning's activities without worrying much about being overheard. In spite of their sense that their conversation was rather secure, they still spoke in carefully chosen phrases, so an overhearing person would not get much of a drift of what they were discussing.

They were both dressed in civilian clothes, and to the surrounding people they could have been business men eating lunch together.

About a fourth of the patrons of the café were sitting outside on a shaded porch. Screens around the perimeter shielded the diners from the hot rays of the noonday sun.

Just as Major Haim reached for another mouthful of hummus with a slice of pita bread, he and Hark were surprised to see a motorcycle with a rider and passenger ride directly into the café through the screened porch and into the interior. As they slid to a stop, the passenger yelled something that Haim could not understand and reached into a backpack that he had pulled off and was holding on his lap.

In a second, there was a blinding flash and a large explosion demolished the café and its patrons. Bodies and body parts were thrown about. Chairs, tables, linens, glasses, plates and supplies were scattered into the air above where the café formerly existed.

Haim and Hark did not hear the explosion. They were mercifully killed instantly. The fireball enveloped the patrons, riders and the motorcycle. Only the frame and a few steel engine parts were found in the rubble, several yards from where they were when the bomb detonated.

Within just a few minutes, sirens and emergency vehicles could be heard converging on the café, or what was left of it. Medical personnel began searching through the smoking rubble for survivors and marking the bodies of those killed for later removal.

Police and security personnel from the Israeli Defense Forces took pictures and made measurements of the scene.

Word of the blast was transmitted by all available means to the IDF and the intelligence forces immediately. Every person in military service tensed up and became even more vigilant. Border crossings into and from the west bank and Gaza were closed. Israel hunkered down in reaction to the disaster.

Preliminary estimates by military and police were that approximately sixty people were killed and more than two hundred injured by the blast.

A few minutes after ten PM local time, Lieutenant Abrams tapped softly on the door opening of General Haim, the Israeli Chief of Staff.

"Yes. What is it Phillip?"

Lieutenant Abrams was visibly shaking. His voice shook, too, as he said, "Sir, it is my sad duty to tell you that it appears that your son Ari was a victim of the blast in Netanya. I am so sorry, sir."

General Haim did not speak. His mouth dropped open. He grabbed his chest and was stunned by the news. Lieutenant Abrams stepped over and drew the shades that let the outside light stream into General Haim's third floor office.

As the General sobbed, Abrams went out and closed the door.

As fate would have it, the day of Ari's funeral, two days later, it rained steadily and was dark gray. Family friends and military men and women related to Ari and to his father, General Tori Haim, swelled the crowd at the cemetery to over a hundred. Wearing a dark Homburg hat and a wig and moustache, President Thompson stepped forward after the burial to extend his personal condolences to General Haim. In a breach of protocol, only two men accompanied the President into the crowd, equally as well disguised. Tori Haim choked when he saw who the tall man really was.

"Oh, Mr. President, how very kind of you to come," he choked out, with tears partially obstructing his vision. President Thompson hugged his friend and patted him on the back. Jefe hugged his old friend and they sobbed together. Lero did not speak to General Haim, both of their eyes were filled with tears. Lero held Haim's hand with both of his, and then, knowing that their friend needed to greet other friends, the President and Lero and Jefe eased back into the crowd and, allowing others to press by, faded to the back of the crowd, where they walked deliberately to a gray Suburban. Once they were confident they could leave without causing a stir, the Suburban slowly motored away.

Forty miles away, and an hour later, a Grumman G-V nosed into the sunset for its trans-Atlantic journey.

Late that night, the Grumman, using its civilian registration number, landed at Reagan International Airport and taxied to the Fixed Base Operator's tarmac. Only a single black Suburban with tinted windows waited at the gate for the President and his abbreviated group. In five minutes they were gone, weaving their way through traffic back to the seat of government.

No one else got off of the plane and as soon as the Suburban departed, it started its engines and taxied to the active runway for its long trip back to Tucson.

When they had gotten away from the airport, the President spoke to his driver: "It was worth it, Charlie. Thanks for setting this up for me. It meant a lot to General Haim for us to be there."

"Any time, Mr. President. It was a privilege to be involved."

Chapter 2

A month later, General Haim seethed with anger. His agents at Mossad had determined, from the shreds of flesh left of the bombers and the motor block of the bike they rode in on, that the perpetrators were from Hezbollah, the party of God, sponsored worldwide by the Islamic Republic of Iran. Over a period of several weeks, General Haim decided to do something about the insult to the state of Israel and to him personally.

It was late afternoon. General Haim mused as he leaned back in his chair. Things were rather quiet in his office complex and it gave him time to think and plan. He thought of his friend Rafi Eitan and the joy it was to work with him . They, together had a long history together in intelligence work. They had been posted by Prime Minister Golda Meir to help set up SAVAK (the Organization of National Security and Information) for the Shah in the early years. With the help of the American CIA, they had organized the structure and hired the original personnel for the Shah. Rafi had done a tour with Shin Bet, the internal security branch of MOSSAD while Tori had been posted to the Political Action and Liaison Department. What he was hoping to put together would be best handled by Kidon, the elite expert assassins of the Caesarea branch, a very dark and super-secret group. Over the years, they had accounted for almost all of the Black September group that had kidnapped and murdered the Olympic athletes in Frankfurt in1972. They killed their way through the group one by one and nothing stood in their way. Tori remembered spending lots of afternoons at the range watching and participating in the training of their marksmen. The most popular weapon was a suppressed .22 automatic, most often a Beretta which could be easily concealed. The men got to where they could place two quick shots very close together after a quick draw from their pockets. They were allowed to start from a position with their hand in their pocked around the grip of the pistol. In just a couple of seconds, they could draw, and more important, place two well-aimed shots on a target seven yards away very reliably.

He remembered when he and Rafi swam ashore from the "fish" (two man submersibles) after being towed by the inflatables up close to the shore. They took the Trojan from the submersible and put it in a waiting delivery truck and then changed into civilian clothes inside. They went into Tripoli and carried the Trojan up three flights of stairs and placed it in an rented apartment where it would remain for six months, receiving and re-broadcasting messages from an Israeli ship in the Mediterranean. It was clever enough to deceive the Americans into believing that Khadafi and his minions had bombed the discotheque in Germany. It did not succeed in fooling the French and Italians, though, so when President Reagan decided to attack Khadafi's compound and headquarters in Libya, the French refused to allow American planes to over-fly France. The resulting attack so rattled Khadafi that he was thereafter much easier to deal with. Tori had been with Rafi and the others, when the Prime Minister had thanked the group and when he gave Rafi his private commendation for conceiving and executing the mission. Now, sadly, Rafi was gone and so were the times they had wreaked such havoc on the enemies of Israel together.

What Tori now had in mind was a lot more massive than a couple of .22 rounds, but the recollection of the efforts of the men and their devotion to Israel remained pleasant memories to him. No, this needed to be just a little bit spectacular and very personal.

The awesome responsibility of his position as Chief of Staff of the Israeli Defense Forces weighed heavily on him sometimes. Now, he had the opportunity to use its assets for a personal project. He knew that even if successful, it would probably cost him his job and his retirement pension, but some things were worth the risk. The reward would be greatly personal, but it would have world-wide ramifications. If he were successful in the mission in chief and thereafter were able to conceal his involvement, it would be one of the best pieces of clandestine work ever.

A Cruise missile is way too slow. A swift fighter could easily overtake it and shoot it down. There would be hundreds of miles between the border and the target for one to do so, too. Nuclear weapons would kill many not innocent, but less guilty people. Need speed, nap of the earth radar, need to hit within one hundred feet of target. Only way, use an F-16, have spotter near target so plane can be directed close enough. Piloted or un-piloted? Laser designator? Escape plan?

At first, General Haim considered stealing a nuclear weapon, but due to the complications of such an attempt, he decided to use a pair of high explosive conventional bombs on an F-16 that could be guided to a precise target and it certainly had the speed. He knew that the Ayatollah had directed the Hezbollah to kill Ari. It was personal. Now, it was his turn. He would need loyal confederates. This could cost all of them their careers, if not their freedom or their lives. These men had to be determined and angry enough to risk it all.

On his way to visit the avionics shop at Ovda to talk to Lt. Mossburg, who ran the unit that installed and serviced the guidance units in the Predator and other drones, General Haim mused about his plan. Mossburg had lost a brother to a Hezbollah attack that just barely failed to kill an Ambassador to Great Britain in London. Five other Israeli security agents were lost along with Mossburg's brother. It was time to hit back. Official channels were bogged down with international niceties. The Prime Minister must be left out of this arrangement for at least two reasons: He would never agree to the strike, and revealing his desire to strike would cause the Prime

Minister to remove Haim from his powerful position, thus disabling the strike before it could take shape, and if the Prime Minister did like the idea of a strike, it could cost the country the support of its most devoted ally. This strike, he understood, could ignite a war that could consume the region in a bitter conflict. The whole geopolitical climate in the area was like a forest in October, after a long hot autumn.   A tinder box, just ready to explode. There was many times enough hatred built up to fuel such an outbreak, and, if it broke open, how many lives would be lost? What borders would remain the same after the conflict as they were now? Perhaps such a war was necessary to re-align the perverse borders imposed on the region after World War II. Those borders seemed to have been designed to create and perpetuate weakness and internal strife. Ethnicity was feared by the designers. Areas like what has become Kurdistan were carved up so that three or four countries shared the population, instead of one cohesive country. Now, all the resentment of the decades since World War II could be unleashed. General Haim thought of these things, but did not really care if he set off a regional firestorm. He wanted the Ayatollah dead. He wanted something "significant" to happen. He wanted the enemy to know that they were being struck in retaliation for killing his son. Only a smoking hole in the earth and concrete would be appropriate. Then, the secondary's surrounding the Ayatollah would be fighting for control of Iran for years, perhaps.

"Whoever they chose or came to the top on his own power would have to remember not to mess with us," he thought. They can fill their streets with crowds shouting "Death to Israel. Death to the Jews," but in their hearts, they will know that they had better not mess with us. They will have to know that we can strike anywhere at any time, and that we will strike if provoked." The Americans had kept the Israelis on a short leash for many, many years, stifling their desire to strike at the Ayatollah and his proxies, Hezbollah and Hamas and all the other independent actors. Now, as far as Haim was concerned, the gloves were off.

As long as the Americans tried to play nice with the mullahs, they would be continuing to press as fast as they could to develop the capability to construct a nuclear device and the delivery capability needed. Delay was clearly on the side of the mullahs. The clock was ticking. The Americans were trading the inevitable necessity of dealing forcefully with the problem in order to have, as Neville

Chamberlin called it "peace in our time." We saw what good that did in 1938. Now eighty five years later, on other turf, the same sort of dance was playing out. Tick, tick, tick.

All these things coursed through his mind as he rode in the rear seat of the air conditioned car on its way to Ovda in the bright, unrelenting sunlight.

Chapter 3

In the second sub-basement bunker near the Army barracks at Ovda, General Haim walked the cool hallway to the second door from the elevator. He opened the door and stepped in. There were five technicians in the Research Technology Department of Mossad working on equipment and electronic devices at separate work stations around the room. Seeing the General, one of them immediately stood, prompting the others to quickly followed suit.

"Relax, men," said Haim, with a wave. "Sorry to have disturbed you. Please carry on. I just want to speak to Lieutenant Mossburg for a moment."

General Haim had known Gabriel since birth. He remembered congratulating his father when Gabriel was born. Gabriel's family had given so much to their country. His father was killed defending the Golan Heights in a Hezbollah uprising in 2001. Gabriel was fit, six feet tall, slender, and late twenties by now.

Out of respect, he came to attention and saluted General Haim. General Haim solemnly returned his salute, then smiled and extended his arms to hug Gabriel, who was the closest thing to a son that Haim now had.

"Do you have a few minutes, Gabriel?" asked General Haim.

"Of course, I do," said Gabriel.

General Haim motioned Gabriel to follow him and the two left the room and walked down the hall to a room on the other side of the hall. General Haim took out a key and opened the door. When he tripped the light switch, Gabriel could see in a nice, but subdued light, a dark conference table and chairs. General Haim took one other than at the head of the table and motioned Gabriel to sit across from him so they could talk eye to eye.

"Thank you, Gabriel, for coming to Ari's funeral and reception. It would have meant a lot to him."

"We were crushed by his death, Sir. It was an honor to attend, but it was a terrible event."

"Yes, it was," said General Haim and paused for a moment to reflect.

"Gabriel, I want to ask you something very important. Your position here at the

Research Technology Department puts you in a position to help me with a project. Before I tell you about it, I must ask that, whether you decide to help me or not, which will be entirely voluntary, you not speak of this conversation again to anyone."

Gabriel, caught somewhat off guard by the General's request, gulped and hesitated for a moment before saying, "If I can help you with anything, sir, you have but to ask."

"Good, Gabriel. Thank you." said Haim.

"We know that the terrorists responsible for Ari's death and the deaths of others that day were from Hezbollah. I don't know if you are aware, but the United States and the state of Israel help the Iranians set up Savak. Things have definitely changed from those days, though. The personnel is diametrically different philosophically, but the structure of SAVAK is the same, with the same divisions of labor. Now that Khomeini's successors are in charge, there is no limit to their hatred of us and our friends across the Atlantic."

General Haim paused a moment, then asked: "Do you think you could equip an F-16 as a drone for a one way mission?"

Gabriel was stunned. Then, as he thought about the question, his mind whirled. He took a full minute to answer.

"No one has tried that, sir, but it could be done. With the use of a satellite, one could control the aircraft from virtually anywhere."

Gabriel paused a moment, then asked: "Uncle Tori, is this an official request?"

"No, Gabriel. This is a special project. Only a very few people will know about this. I need to tell you that this could cost you your commission and would always be on your record. If you would rather not get involved, that will be fine with me, since you have given me your word that you will never speak of this conversation to anyone else. Think if over and call me tomorrow on the secure line to tell me your answer. Now, I must go. Thank you for talking with me. We will see each other much more often in the future, I hope."

They both rose and left the secure room. Gabriel went back into the laboratory and Haim went up the elevator to the scorching heat of a southern Israeli afternoon.

The next day, late in the afternoon, his aide told General Haim that there was a phone call for him on the secure line. When he answered, Gabriel's voice responded.

"Uncle, I would be honored to be included in your project. I will be expecting instructions when you are ready. Thank you."

"Good, Gabriel," said Haim. "I will be in touch." Both men hung up. Each pondered what they had just done.

Chapter 4

General Haim had his driver stop outside the hangar. He told the driver he could wait in the shade inside if he wanted, because he might be a while.

The hangar was dimly lit; it seemed, at first, because of the change from the blinding light of the torrid desert day. Haim walked to the southwest corner of the hangar. There was a small office with an old air conditioner humming in the window.

When Haim stepped in, the officer, who had one of his feet on top of an open drawer of his desk, leaped to his feet and came to attention.

"Easy, Yakob, you will break something with such efforts. Be at ease, please."

Major Yakob Steiner had leaped to his feet when he saw the stars on the uniform of his unexpected visitor, but now realized that the man before him was his longtime friend, General Haim.

"Sorry sir, for the stir. Just wanted to show proper respect for the uniform," he said, beginning to relax from his position at attention.

"Sit with me a minute, Yakob," said Haim, pointing to his chair.

When both had settled into their chairs, Haim leaned across the desk and, looking Yakob directly in the eyes, asked, "Do you think you could get me an old F-16 for a one way mission, off the books?"

Yakob's eyes bulged.

"Sir, we have twenty seven F-16s here at Ovda. Some of the older ones have more than ten thousand hours on them. Let me look at the list."

He went to the nearby board on the wall and pulled off a clip board and returned to his seat.

"We have three that are high engine time and due to be de-activated sometime soon. My commanding officer has to decide how many to ask the Americans to refurbish and how many to second to National Guard Units or other friendly air forces."

"The highest time aircraft we have is number 435. The engine is near half time between overhauls and it is a sound aircraft, but it had the misfortune of having made a gear up landing and everyone is very wary of it now. It is structurally sound, though. No real damage was done. The gear failed to deploy due to a stuck hydraulic valve."

"Number 606 is next, with an engine that is about three fourths of the way to overhaul. It is a sound aircraft, with no damage history. It has the oldest radios in the fleet, though."

Haim studied for a moment, then asked, "Where are these two aircraft now, Yakob?"

Yakob flipped over the sheet for 435.

"435 is here at Ovda in a revetment on the north end of the field. It has not flown is over a year. The revetment is in good condition and the doors are locked."

"606 is with the First Squadron at Hatzor Airbase east of Tel Aviv. It is technically "on the line," but it is not one the pilots favor and it has not flown in six months."

Haim studied for a moment, then asked: "I want to involve you in something off the books. There is danger and the possibility that we all could lose our commissions. Since you were a close friend of Ari's, I want you to be involved if you want. If you choose not to, I don't want you to discuss this with anyone else ever. Is that OK?"

"Sure," said Yakob. "Does this have anything to do with Ari's death?"

"Yes," said Haim. "We have decided to let the Ayatollah know how vulnerable he is. Actually, he will not have much time to think about what is happening, but his survivors will put the pieces together and, in time, will figure out who did what was done. I want them to know they mess with us at their peril."

"Good, General Haim. Count me in. Let me know what you expect from me and I will get on it."

"Fine, Yakob," said Haim. "I will be back in touch when I get a few other things arranged. Expect to hear from me within a week. Take care of yourself and give my best regards to you wife."

"Will do, sir. And I will not discuss this with anyone, including my wife."

"That will be fine, Yakob. See you soon."

General Haim found his driver sitting in a folding chair, watching the door that Haim came out of. They walked together back to the car that was baking in the sun.

Chapter 5

Haim met again with Yakob a couple of weeks later.

"Do you think you could find a couple of thousand pound dumb bombs with contact fuses for our project? Surely there must be a couple in the bunkers that would not be missed."

"Why don't we use smart bombs," asked Yakob. "They would be useful perhaps if the primary guidance system went awry or was damaged by defenders."

"I thought it might be too difficult to appropriate two such expensive and scarce pieces of ordnance, Yakob. Am I correct?"

"If we used the locked revetment on the north end of the field, we can work on 435 secretly to get it ready. I am the only one who controls the keys to the revetment. I think I know where we can get a couple of smart bombs whose absence will not be noticed before we use them."

"Yakob, for your protection, I will not tell you the identity of the others involved in this project. Likewise, they will not know your identity, either. Please make no effort to acquire their names and they have been instructed not to attempt to acquire yours. There are very few men involved. They are all IDF people and are personally known by me and me alone. I will want you to leave the key to the revetment in a hiding place where they can pick it up. Only if necessary will they identify themselves to you and will do so by giving the code word: Gladius. You may expect to be contacted by someone in the next few days. They will work in the revetment at night, using night vision goggles, to specially fit the aircraft. When they are nearing completion, I will alert you so you can tell us how to acquire the bombs. I want you to find a maintenance mechanic to go over the aircraft, someone known only to you and in whom you have absolute confidence, to check out the aircraft and get it ready. You will need to find some external drop tanks to expand the fuel capacity, also. Will that be feasible, Yakob?"

"There are enough drop tanks over at the Training Battalion that we can borrow a couple without detection, I think," said Yakob.

"Yakob, by necessity, I choose to keep you in the dark about many details of this mission. If we fail, you will probably not hear any more about this mission. If we succeed, you will read about it in the newspapers and it is possible that you and I will never speak of it again, but I thank you for your loyalty to me personally and to Israel for doing this."

It was twenty three hundred hours, according to the log of the gate personnel when the six by six truck arrived. It was logged in as returning to base from a transport mission, but later investigation determined that that particular truck had never been to Ovda before.

The gate guards checked inside the truck and found the correct number of marked crates called for on the manifest.

After it cleared the gate, the truck drove to the southernmost road on the base and loitered slowly as it wound its way back through the buildings and barracks of Ovda. After determining that they were probably not being followed, the truck went north and approached the closed revetment. As it stopped outside, a single soldier, using a flashlight, went up to the doors and inserted a corroded brass key. After a few attempts, he got the padlock to yield and opened the doors. The truck promptly pulled in next to the aircraft and shut down. It was all done quickly and quietly. The men waiting in the revetment and the arriving men unloaded the crates from the trucks. It was heavy work and took over an hour, since there were only four of them. They each had a name placard on their uniforms, but with noms de guerre and not their real names. Once they were finished, the arriving crew went into the office to bunk out for a few hours and would leave the base in the early hours of morning to ostensibly return to their base.

The avionics crewmen worked on through the night.

"Where will you be while you pilot the drone?" asked General Haim.

"We could do it from the revetment here. I could mount an antenna on the roof out of sight. We will have plenty of room once the plane is gone, too. We could stockpile food and water and even have a port-a-potty in there so we would not need to leave during the mission."

"Have you calculated routes and times yet?" asked Haim.

"I have looked at some routes, but I wanted to talk with you to get some guidance before I calculated times and distances. From your standpoint, are there any restrictions or matters that need to be considered in planning the route?" asked Yakob.

"How are you going to get the plane from the revetment to the runway?" asked Haim.

"Actually, there is only one left turn out front of the revetment and then it could taxi all the way to the active runway, however, it would be about a thousand feet from the northerly threshold. There would be over nine thousand feet from there to the south. No need to turn to the north and go to that end of the runway. We could depart from the intersection. If this plane cannot get off in nine thousand feet, we are sunk anyway.," said Yakob.

"How are we going to file a flight plan for this flight, General?" asked Yakob. "How much range should I plan for?"

"I have an agent in the air traffic control center who can file a bogus flight plan with forged signatures. I will take care of that. As far as the tower guys are concerned, it will be a normal night training departure," said Haim.

"Plan on a range of eighteen hundred kilometers."

"Good plan," said Yakob.

"Pardon my curiosity, General, but how are you going to tell the aircraft exactly where you want it to hit? We can program the smart bombs easily enough, but if you plan to crash the plane into the target, how do you plan to guide the plane the last mile or so?" asked Yakob.

"We must have the range I told you because the target may be anywhere within an arc that is about nine hundred kilometers long. I don't want to go into more detail for your sake, Yakob. My plan is to use personnel on the ground with a laser designator so the plane can hit the exact spot we want to hit," said Haim.

"Do you have the personnel matter taken care of?" asked Yakob.

"Yes, but I don't want to tell you any more, for your own protection and welfare, Yakob," said Haim.

"I understand, sir. What is your time goal for this flight?"

"We are not in any particular hurry. I want you to take as much time as you need to be ready. Do you think you could be ready in a month?" asked Haim.

"I think so," said Yakob. "The longer we spend in preparation, the more likely we are to be discovered, though. However, most of the men here know better than to get too curious. There have been so many secret missions launched from Ovda, that the men know better than to make much of a locked door with lights on inside. If someone thinks something is going on in the revetment, he knows to speak to his superior officer. His superior officer will tell him to leave it alone and keep clear of it and to forget he said anything."

"Exactly," said Haim. "Let's try for a month and adjust if we need to. Do you need some cash for equipment and bribes?" asked Haim.

"It would be nice to have some reserve, just in case," said Yakob.

"Take this," said Haim, as he handed Yakob a manila envelope about an inch thick.

Yakob was startled, but smoothly took the envelope from Haim's grasp.

Chapter 6

Two days later, General Haim was ending a long day of staff meetings with higher level officers when his aide whispered to him that he had a call on his secure phone.

"Hello," said General Haim.

Yakob, said, "General, would you prefer to use a Mirage IIIE instead of the F-16? I have one nearby that would make an ideal candidate. We grabbed it on that last dust up with the Palestinians at an airport in Sinai. It still has all the Egyptian markings, too."

"That might be a better aircraft for our purposes," said the General. "I will call you back."

The next morning, Yakob received a call on the normal line. The caller simply said, "Call the general," and hung up.

Yakob went to the base commander's building when he went for lunch at the mess hall. He went into the air traffic control center office, where it was completely normal for him to appear and walked to an unused desk in a far corner of the room. He picked up the receiver and punched the red button at the right end of the row of buttons. The receiver remained silent for about six seconds, then there was a distinct click, then a normal dial tone. He dialed the number he had memorized."

The phone rang three times and then it was picked up. The voice on the other end said merely, "Hello."

"Redhawk calling to speak to Falcon," he said.

There was silence on the other end for about thirty seconds, then he heard the familiar voice of General Haim.

"Yes, what is it?" he asked in a normal voice.

"Sir, we have a Mirage IIIE in another revetment that we could use if you want to use something other than an F-16. I am a bit concerned that identification might be easier if the F-16 were used. If this is a concern, the numbers throughout the Mirage could be obliterated and it would be very difficult to tell where it came from. "

"This sounds like a good alternative. Let me think about it and I will get back in touch. Thank you." He hung up.

Haim used his laptop computer to look up the specifications for the Mirage IIIE.

"With roughly fifteen thousand pounds of useful load, including fuel, it has the carrying capacity we need," he thought. "Eight hard points on the wings. Hang a bomb and a fuel tank on each side, and still stay within maximum take off weight, even with all the on board fuel tanks full. Plenty of speed, too," he thought.

Chapter 7

So many of the days at Tucson are hot and dry, it is difficult to tell the season passage. It was a cool day for Tucson, though. Late September, Lero and Jefe were working on organization at the office. They had reviewed all of the "projects" and the "budget proposal" for the coming fiscal year. Next they would review the personnel situation to see if any additional persons were needed for the missions already in the planning stages.

It was shortly before 6 PM. Velma, the office manager, was almost ready to leave. She worked normally from ten to 6 due to the heat and it was convenient for her. Her children could be gotten off to school and a few errands run before she needed to report in the morning, and her long time live in boyfriend, Karl, would be watching over the kids and fixing dinner for the family.

When the intercom came on, Jefe assumed that she was letting him know that she was leaving for the day, but instead, she said, "There is a Mr. Murfree here to see you, sir."

Jefe was startled. This was most unusual, but he gathered his composure and said to her, "Show him in, Velma, and you may go."

Jefe and Lero both got to their feet as the door opened and in stepped President Thompson.

"Sorry to drop in like this, fellows, but I was passing over and decided to talk to you both. Can we visit a few minutes?"

"Of course," said Jefe, deftly concealing his surprise.

The President took a chair in front of Jefe's desk next to Lero.

"I know you both are deep into year-end planning and budgetary matters, but I need to alert you, eye to eye about a situation. This is most secret and I chose not to communicate by electronic means. How long has it been since this room was swept?"

"Last Monday, sir," said Lero, who spoke for the first time.

The President turned slightly, so he could look at both of them as he spoke.

"As you know, we have assets in foreign countries that try to discover items of interest and let us know about them promptly. In this case, it is not an adversary that the information comes from. We have a thread of information to the effect that an ally is planning a preemptory strike on an as yet undetermined target in Iran."

He paused to let the information sink in, to let the wheels in Jefe's head and Lero's head whirl a bit.

"After our strike two years ago with the Vulcan bomber, the Iranians have rebuilt their facilities and relocated some manufacturing and processing activities. We remain convinced that, no matter what they have or will agree to in public, they intend to press forward with all due dispatch to acquire the capability to produce a nuclear weapon and an appropriate regional delivery system."

He continued, "Superimposed on their rush toward production, is our concern that matters in the area will boil over. As you know, ISIS has the middle east in turmoil. Millions of refugees have been displaced in Syria, Iraq and Lebanon. The news networks are absorbed with ISIS and have placed much less emphasis on the concern that Iran will go nuclear."

"We believe that Iran is taking advantage of the distraction to build more facilities and to move the manufacturing machinery that is most vulnerable to attack to better facilities underground."

"I realize that we have several "projects" currently under way, but do you both have time to give this matter your attention?" he asked.

Jefe spoke first. "Sir, we do have "projects" under way, as you know, but both Lero and I are at your service. The "projects" are capable of running themselves with very little input from us. This will change in about a month, when we intend to exfiltrate a team of agents from central Iran. We also have a team of observers in Ukraine who must be retrieved sometime soon, but there is no immediate need to do that and it can be handled by our team's desk officer who is completely capable of overseeing it."

"Good," said President Thompson. "Our people at the NSA and the National Radio Observatory have picked up some transmissions on a frequency not previously used by the Ayatollah's guys that concerns us, too, but the main thing I want you to concentrate on is finding out more about the possibility that something is going on."

"How do you want us to go about this, Mr. President," asked Lero.

"Jefe, since you and Alita have that villa on Keros, it might be nice if you would stop and see General Haim on your next visit. Just play it that you are on an extended vacation while Lero is learning what is necessary to run this unit. Take Alita with you. Just see if Tori will let you in on anything. Report to me in writing. Do not transmit anything by any electronic means. A FedEx letter will reach me in less than twenty four hours, so use that, and use the V-26 code for sensitive items. Address it to Mr. Murfree at the Alexandria address, and sign it 'Eddie.'"

"If you do not ferret out anything, just return to Keros and stand by to be contacted. I want you, Lero, to follow up by visiting with General Haim about ten or twelve days later. You may tell him that you are on your way to Kuwait to meet a "contractor" for a "project" and just wanted to stop by and visit, to express your personal condolences for the loss of his son."

"I get the medical reports on both of you, so I know that the sawbones is satisfied that you, Lero, have recovered completely from your head wound, but that is a medical decision. Do you sense that you have any impediment of any kind?" he asked, looking directly, not sternly but with concern, at Lero.

"As far as I can tell, sir, I have no impediments. My ophthalmologist fit me for new glasses last month and I asked her especially, to be on the lookout for any damage. She said she found none. My eyesight is unaffected by the wound. I notice no other sensory or motor deficit. Jean says I am every bit as difficult as before, too," said Lero.

They all chuckled at the last remark. Jefe and the President knew how devoted Jean and Lero were to each other. Jean was now a full-fledged member of the team and they all trusted her judgment and candor completely.

I want you both to travel by using one of our transports, if possible, on these trips. Stage out of Athens. I will alert our people there that they may be called upon to assist you. Let me hear from you, Lero, the same way as from Jefe. Sign your report, Brice, please. I know it is near the end of the fiscal year. Do you have enough funds to comfortably do this?"

Jefe said, "Yes, sir, we are comfortable in the money department for now. If you have time to do so, we could arrange dinner in a private room adjacent to the mess hall."

"That would be great. I can sleep on the plane on the way back. I have to meet with the Chairman of the House Appropriations Committee at eight tomorrow morning."

He swung up out of his chair and they all went out together. Jefe and Lero recognized the two men waiting at the car from their earlier trips to Washington. President Thompson told them both to go get a good dinner in the mess hall once they had him and Jefe and Lero safely in the private dining room. Once they were satisfied that the situation was secure, the officers went, one at a time and got a dinner tray, but they sat together where they could keep an eye on the door to the private dining room.

Chapter 8

Lieutenant Yakob Steiner eyed the spec chart for the Mirage IIIE. The non-negotiable part of the payload was the two smart bombs that would weigh one thousand pounds each. Otherwise, he could load as much fuel as the design would allow. If he used the 1700 liter drop tank that would fit the IIIE and 50 and 500 models, he could add almost three hundred miles (485 kilometers) to the range. What this aircraft was going to lack in terms of armament would be made up for in scat. With a maximum speed of over fourteen hundred miles per hour, it could outrun almost anything. Even with the bombs still aboard, after dropping the drop tank in the desert, it could make good speed. Such speed would give it a big advantage in the run into the target. Even if radar picked it up, this aircraft would be able to close on the target at nearly Mach 2. Defending aircraft would have to be very lucky to be in the proper position and going in the same direction to have a chance at overtaking it. Even an antiaircraft missile would have a difficult time overtaking it in time to prevent its strike. The best part is that it was an Egyptian aircraft, seized during the "difficulties" in the Sinai the last summer and no one outside of a very few men knew they had the aircraft. It was in another locked revetment on the north of the field. As far as he could tell, and he would know, since he was the officer in charge of aircraft availability and all locked revetments were under his control, no one had been in the revetment where it was since it was originally sealed.

Chapter 9

Lero's cell phone rang in his pocket. He stopped by a display in the store and answered it. After he said "Hello," the voice on the other end said, "This is Mr. Murfree. Say the word, please."

Lero looked around and saw no one close enough to overhear him and said "Houston" into the phone.

"Hope I did not interrupt anything," said Mr. Murfree.

"No, sir," said Lero. "Just doing a little last minute Christmas shopping after the seminar. Expect to leave for home base tonight."

"What is your '20' (Note: this is code for location)?" asked Mr. Murfree.

"I am in the shopping mall just off of Water Street, in Morgantown, West Virginia. I have been here at an Aerospace Seminar to renew my Airline Transport Pilot Certificate."

"Good that you are close," said Mr. Murfree. "Janice and I are at Camp David, just a few miles east of you. Could you come by before you go back to home base?"

"Of course, sir," said Lero. "Do you want me to come right away, like this evening?"

"That would be fine, if you could. I hate to delay your return to Jean by having you stay overnight and come tomorrow."

"She will be fine with it, sir. I will rent a car and be over in about two hours."

"Good, see you then. Thanks."

Lero hung up and grabbed up the bags of his shopping selections and walked out to the street. Cabs were waiting for fares in the December night, with their exhausts steaming in the breeze. He got in the first one and said, "Take me to the Morgantown Airport, please."

The Avis lady was just about to close the counter when he walked in.

"Do you have any cars available?"

"Yes, sir, I have two left. You can have a Chevy sedan or a Ford Fusion sedan."

"I'll take the Ford, please," said Lero, as he produced his driver's license and credit card.

As she was inputting his information into her desk top computer, she casually asked why he chose the Ford over the Chevrolet.

"Because Ford did not take any bail out money," he said.

She nodded knowingly and said: "I did not mean to be nosey, but the company likes me to survey renters to see if there is anything we can pick up that might promote better service."

"I always choose Avis when I can," he said. "Your ad campaign years ago about being second and having to try harder stuck with me."

She smiled and handed him his keys and the contract. She pointed to the door at her left and he went on with a nod and a smile. "Have a safe trip. It is snowy on the mountains tonight."

He thanked her and opened the door into a snow squall.

It was only a few miles back to the Interstate from the airport, just down the road toward Cheat Lake. Once on the Interstate, he set the cruise control for seventy and motored over the Appalachian peak into Maryland. Holiday traffic was sparse, but moving along briskly. He made good time in spite of the blowing snow and pulled up to the front security gate at Camp David in an hour and thirty three minutes.

"Good evening," he said to the inquisitive guard. "Lero, to see the President."

"Just a moment, sir," said the guard and went back into the guard station while his armed back up kept eyes on Lero and the car he was in.

In a moment, the guard returned with a device that resembled a portable police radar.

"Look directly into the lenses, sir, and try not to blink for at least ten seconds, please."

While this was taking place a guard with a bomb sniffing dog inspected the car, even using a lighted mirror to look at the underside.

"Right," said Lero as he looked into the retina scanner.

In a few seconds, the guard withdrew the device and waited, looking at the display on the back side. In about eight seconds, it blinked a green light, and since it had been pre-set with Lero's name, that meant that the ID was confirmed.

"You can go ahead, sir, take the left fork ahead and it is the second building on the right."

"Thanks," said Lero, and motored up the narrow blacktop road.

As he pulled into the lot adjacent to the second building, he was greeted by two security guards. He got out of the car as they approached.

"Good evening, sir. Name please," one said.

"My name is Lero. I am expected."

"Right, sir, just hold still while we wand you."

Lero stood still while they ran the electronic wand over him. No masses of metal were detected, so they approved him. The one who spoke earlier said, "You are good to go, sir. The guard at the door will direct you."

"Thanks, fellows," said Lero and walked up the path to the "cabin." Even though it was of log construction, it was quite a bit more than a log cabin. It was, in fact, a large one story house, specially built for President Eisenhower in the 1950s. It had weathered well, and was constantly maintained in top shape.

He stepped in as instructed by the guard. The President was waiting for him in the entry hall, dressed in jeans and a sweater, his favorite off duty attire.

"Good to see you," said the President, extending a hand. "I hope this meeting will not be too much of a disruption in your schedule."

"Good to see you again, too, sir. No problem with my schedule."

Lero noticed that there was a nice fire in the fireplace in the lounge. He followed the President in.

"Are you thirsty?" asked the President.

"I am fine, sir," said Lero.

"Would you drink an O'Douls with me?" asked the President.

"Sure, that sounds good," said Lero.

Neither the President nor Lero drank alcohol, but both appreciated the taste of a cold beer after a long day. O'Douls was the President's favorite non-alcoholic beer and Lero had come to appreciate it, too, when they met.

Since they were alone, the President went to the little refrigerator built into the book case behind him and retrieved two bottles.

He and Lero sat down at a round pine table that had been made of wood from the trees around the cabin. It was at least sixty years old, and had the patina of good care.

The President clinked his bottle with Lero's and looked directly at him.

"I know I have asked you to do some sensitive and dangerous stuff. I want you to know, just between us, how much I appreciate you and your service."

"Sir, it is a privilege to serve, besides, I really enjoy the work. The people you have associated me with are a constant source of encouragement and they give me great confidence."

"I am glad you like your work, Lero. You guys mean a lot to me. The reason I called you up here in this cold evening is so I can brief you on a project. It is so sensitive that I wanted to talk to you only about it. Jefe will be sent to take care of part of the assignment, but you and you alone will know the full extent of the mission. I trust Jefe completely, but with modern chemical interrogation techniques, only those who know something can reveal it."

"Here is what is afoot. You remember last August, when General Haim's son and his exec were killed by the suicide bomber? Well, our friend has, through his excellent intelligence people, determined that it was not just a terrorist act, but a deliberate plan by the highest authorities in Iran, part of a plan to demoralize Haim and distract him as well as to punish him for his efficient destruction of the terror networks that Iran has in the middle east that are a constant threat to the safety of the Israelis. Our friend has determined to strike back and has a "project" under way to kill the Ayatollah."

The President hesitated to let the last part sink in. Lero did not change expression, but the President knew that the wheels were whirling behind those eyes.

"Do you know how he intends to go about it, sir?" asked Lero.

"Yes. I have told no one before, but I have an asset who is very close to Tori and reports directly to me."

"It seems," he continued, "that Tori plans to use a seized Mirage IIIE fighter that they got from an Egyptian airport during the last skirmish in the Sinai. He plans to use it as a drone and fly it into the building or vehicle where the Ayatollah is. Since the Ayatollah travels a good bit, but observes strict security, his whereabouts are very difficult to detect. Tori has an asset that is in the Ayatollah's entourage and is depending on him to tell him where the Ayatollah is from time to time and what his travel plans are. Tori plans to have an agent infiltrate Iran and be where the Ayatollah plans to be at the appropriate time. He will use a laser designator to paint the building or vehicle where the Ayatollah is and the electronics guys will fly the plane, loaded with bombs, into the building or vehicle."

The President halted to let this information be processed.

"Their reasoning is that a cruise missile is too slow and a squad of special ops guys would not be able to travel fast enough to keep up with the Ayatollah. So, with the information from the source, they will have their agent in place near where the Ayatollah is expected and, if the agent is able to determine that the Ayatollah is, indeed, in a certain building or vehicle, the agent will paint the building or vehicle and the drone will be able to follow the beam to the target."

The President halted again, to give Lero a chance to respond.

"It seems like an event that could upset the whole area, sir. If the Iranians suspect that the Israelis are behind this, it could set off a regional military conflict, perhaps even the use of nuclear weapons. Something like that could spread very quickly and get out of control. World War One started with an assassination, too, as you know. This is very serious."

"I was confident you would see the potential for a much larger problem that this could cause. From your prospective, how would you approach the problem?" asked the President.

"Well, sir, it depends. Do you want us to interfere or de-rail the strike?"

Lero waited while the President took a sip of O'Douls.

The President looked directly at Lero when he replied: "No, I want you to make sure he succeeds."

There was a long pause. Lero took a sip of beer and pondered what he had heard.

"How soon do you think this will all take place, sir?" asked Lero.

"They are up-fitting the Mirage at Ovda as we speak. I expect they have a man ready to take a laser designator with him and penetrate Iran right away. I want you to leave as soon as you return to your base and get equipped. We will arrange transport for you and your team from there. We will supply you with a laser designator the same as the Israelis will be using, so you can paint the Ayatollah if they fail. I know that Jefe and I have repeatedly told you that you will not be placed in a position of danger again, but I really need you to do this. I cannot think of a more qualified person. You speak Arabic and Farsi and with a beard you would look enough like an Iranian to pull this off. I want someone mature enough to look unlikely to be hostile and mature enough to plan as you go. Our equipment people will be in touch and will have what we anticipate you will need ready for you as you go. We can talk more about details in the morning. The steward outside the door will take you to a comfortable room for tonight and we can discuss this some more at breakfast. Thanks again for coming on such short notice. I am grateful. See you in the morning."

Chapter 10

They got up and the President went to the door and left and the steward then stepped in. The steward picked up Lero's suitcase and led him to a room for the night.

The steward tapped on the door at 6:30 AM. Lero answered with "Come in."

"Can you meet the President and First Lady for breakfast at 7, sir?" he asked.

"Sure. Thanks for the heads up," said Lero as he walked quickly toward the shower.

The dining room, as one might expect, was larger than a normal dining room for such a structure. It was homey, with log walls and a knotty pine paneled ceiling. The President and Mrs. Thompson were seated as Lero was escorted in. They both rose to greet him.

"So nice of you to visit with us here, Lero," said Janice Thompson.

"It is always a pleasure to see you both," said Lero as he returned her handshake.

"What do you prefer for breakfast?" asked the President.

"I usually have bran flakes with sliced peaches and one percent milk, but I will have whatever you are having, sir," said Lero.

"We are having scrambled eggs, link sausages, raisin bread toast and orange juice," said Mrs. Thompson.

"Sounds wonderful, count me in," said Lero.

The silver compote steamed as she removed the top to pass it to him.

Lero asked how their children were doing. Mrs. Thompson replied: "Brice is at Southern Miss, in his third year and doing well. Sandy is at Sweet Brier in her first year. They seem to be doing just fine, thanks. We are still getting used to being empty nesters, though. How is Jean?"

"Jean is fine," he said. "She makes my life complete. I am so glad I met her," said Lero.

"We think of you both in Tucson often. Do you both enjoy the desert climate?" she asked.

"Yes, even though I am an Appalachian, I love the desert. We are so grateful to be there," said Lero.

"How will you return there from here?" the President asked.

"I will catch a commercial flight once we finish our business here," he said.

"Why don't you return to Washington with us by helicopter?" asked the President. "It will give us more time to talk and you can catch a flight from Reagan or Dulles. I can have our people return the rental car."

"That would be fine, sir," said Lero with a grin, as he helped himself to a large portion of scrambled eggs.

On the ride back to Andrews, the President showed Lero the designs for a guidance system for bombs that could be attached to the nose and tail of existing one thousand pound bombs. One type had rather normal fins and a glide range of sixty kilometers when dropped from thirty thousand feet and at cruise speed. The other had short wings instead of fins and had a glide distance of one hundred kilometers. Lero showed interest in the designs and asked the President if our country planned on asking the Israeli government, which had published the brochure, if we could use the design. The President said; "Your first mission was the proving ground for these bomb guidance systems. Those four bombs your guys dropped all hit within six feet of the target center. We agreed with the Israelis to share the designs and both we and they will be producing these guidance systems in the near future. They call the concept 'Spice' which stands for Smart, Precise, Impact, Cost Effective. Take this brochure with you and show Jefe and your guys. Keep it in a safe place."

As he finished, they could see that the terrain below indicated that they were approaching the city. Ahead through the open door to the flight deck, they could see the long white runways of Andrews Air Force Base southeast of Washington, D.C. They were approaching from the west, having flown more directly south than directly over the city.

Flashing lights ahead indicated the instrument landing system was operating for an approaching aircraft. The helicopter approached the airport at almost a right angle to the runways and settled onto the tarmac at a marked circle.

When they deplaned, the President went first, as is protocol. He was immediately greeted by an Air Force Colonel who engaged him in emphatic conversation. Mrs. Thompson and Lero exited the helicopter together. He offered her a hand down the stairway. She took his arm as they walked across the breezy tarmac.

She said: "It is a bit embarrassing for me that I cannot know your real name. I just want you to know that the President places immense trust and confidence in you and Jefe and your people."

"Thank you, ma'am, we and all the military personnel are so grateful to have a Commander in Chief who respects us and has our back. Those last eight years were a nightmare for service personnel. Now, the spirit is back and the strength is back in our spines.   He is a great patriot and the men would follow him anywhere."

"Thank you, Lero, and you must stop calling me ma'am. My name is Janice."

"If the name 'Lero' is uncomfortable, you can call me Dan Roman," he said as they watched out the window.

"Is that your real name?" she asked.

"No, it is my 'traveling name,' when I need to use a civilian name rather than my nom de guerre."

"Better, but not perfect," she said. "I guess it will have to do." She smiled at him.

They were now looking out through the large windows as the President finished his conversation with the officer and was walking toward the doors.

"One more thing, if I may," said Mrs. Thompson. "I am an only child. I have no sisters and no close friends just now. The only females I get to talk to are the wives of the men with whom my husband must work and associate. They are not at all those I would choose to be my friends, besides they are all politicians, anyway. Would it be alright if I called Jean to visit, just between us girls? I found her especially easy to talk to while you were conferring with the President last fall. We really hit it off, so to speak."

"I am sure she would love that, Janice. She is a great supporter for me and a good friend. She would love it if you would call. For security purposes, what name will you use?"

"Tell her to expect a call from Daphne, and thanks," she said and she reached to take the arm of her husband.

The President turned to speak to Lero and extended his hand.

"Thanks again for everything you do. I will keep you in touch. Say hello to Jean for us. The Colonel will get you a ride to Tucson right away. Thanks again."

The President and Mrs. Thompson walked to the waiting limousine and Lero watched them through the big windows of the airport lobby.

An airman, actually a female airman, came up to him and asked: "What name should I use for the tickets to Tucson, sir?"

"Dan Roman, thanks," said Lero.

(Note to the detail inclined: Lero chose to use the name Dan Roman as his traveling name. Dan Roman was the co-pilot in the book and movie "The High and Mighty," played by John

Wayne. Those who fly usually get goose bumps just thinking about Ernest K. Gann's masterpiece, and that night flight over the Pacific.)

He sat and watched as a light snow began to fall on the tarmac.

In a few minutes, she returned and said: "We have you booked on a Southwest Airlines flight leaving Dulles in an hour, to Dallas-Fort Worth, with a connection to Tucson. You could be home by dawn."

"Wonderful," said Lero. "Thanks a lot."

"A driver will take you right away. They have your bag in the car already. It is the dark blue Suburban at the end of the walkway. Good luck, sir."

"Thanks again," said Lero and walked to the car with a spring in his step.

Chapter 11

As part of his "easing down" program, Jefe left the office at noon. Lero and he had spent the morning going over the various "projects" that were under way and dictating reports to Mr. Murfree to be typed and mailed in the secure pouch later. All urgent reports or consultations took place over secure satellite phones when available or regular cell phones when necessary.

He stopped by his favorite wine shop and browsed for a couple of cases of favorites and some new ones to try. He bought a couple cases of Moet champagne and a case of Napoleon brandy for good measure. The cases almost filled the trunk, but there would be plenty of room on the plane.

His house was in a nice neighborhood and had an open front yard, but a tall fence gave the back yard plenty of privacy. Eastern ivy had a hard time clinging to the wall and to live in the desert climate of Tucson, but with the automated irrigation system he had installed, it got along just fine.

He did not see Alita when he entered, so he rang the small brass bell at the foot of the stairs to tell her that he was home. Since she did not sing out right away, he surmised that she might be out at the pool, but when he looked out the window, he could not see her. He left his briefcase on the sofa. He went out the double doors onto the back veranda and walked toward the pool.

"Anybody home?" he called.

"Over here," came her voice. She had been sunbathing in the nude and had put two turned over deck chairs on either side of her to shield herself in spite of the tall fence. When she sat up, a wave went through him. My, she was gorgeous. She had on her favorite sunglasses and a hat to shield her face from too much sun, but she was otherwise covered with her favorite coconut butter suntan lotion and glowed beautifully in the afternoon sun.

"I think I might have dozed off in the sun," she said. "It is so lovely here."

As she sat on the air mattress, she said, in a teasing manner: "You really must get more sun, darling. You look so pale. Why don't you join me for a sun bath?"

As he peeled off his shirt, she came over to him. What a sensory adventure it was to watch her walk, nude, in the bright Arizona sun, directly to him. Because of the oil on her, she did not hug him, but leaned up and gave him a very efficient kiss.

There were no noises or other interferences to break their concentration on each other. Luckily, the sun was hot enough to wake them afterward so they did not get too sunburned. They went in and showered off the oil and lingered in the shower a long time.

As he fixed dinner for them, she sat on a straight backed stool at the kitchen island. He had just dumped the stir fry vegetables in the fry pan when he came over to her and sat down opposite her.

"Mr. Murfree wants me to call on a gentleman in the Mediterranean area. He said it would be handy for him if we would hang out at Keros afterward for a while in case he needs me to do something else. Do you think you could stand a little Greek cooking and sunshine for a while?"

She grinned largely. "Could we make love on the terrace next to the pool a lot?" she asked.

"To the extent of our capabilities, my dear. I stocked up on wine, champagne and brandy on the way home. We can take some with us and stock up on food when we get there."

She reached across and squeezed his wrist with a tremendous smile.

"When do we need to leave?" she asked.

"In the next couple of days," he said. "I will catch us a ride on one of the flights and we will go on their schedule. Take enough gear to stay a while."

"I may need to go into town and buy some new clothes once we get there, you know," she said with a sly smile.

"As long as you wear them sparingly, my dear, you can get a new wardrobe if you want," he said.

The smell of the garlic in the stir fry distracted him and he turned back to the stove to complete dinner preparations. While he did so, she opened a bottle of their favorite California Merlot.

Chapter 12

His personal secretary, Kahlil Samir, looked up as the Grand Ayatollah entered his office. Kahlil waited for the Ayatollah to approach and speak, having been told repeatedly that the Ayatollah has weighty matters of religion and politics on his mind constantly and should only be engaged in conversation when the Ayatollah clearly indicates that he wishes to converse.

He went to the barred window of his office and scanned the panorama of Tehran. This office was a mile or so from his official ceremonial office, for security reasons. The ceremonial office, while fully staffed and functioning, was an appendage of this office, and existed as much as a decoy as a functioning branch of government.

(NOTE: All conversations are translated to English from Farsi).

After musing for a few minutes, he asked, "Kahlil, do you have the schedule for next week's trip?"

Kahlil said, "Yes Holiness, it is right here," and he walked the clipboard to him at the window. The Grand Ayatollah squinted at the schedule for a minute or so without comment.

"It is well laid out from north to south and we should be able to keep to the time schedule if the units I will visit are properly prepared," he said.

"Would you like to speak to General Aziz to discuss the preparations?" Kahlil asked, trying to anticipate his wishes.

"Maybe later, Kahlil. Just now, I want to sit and study the schedule and reflect on what I must do at each stop on the list. Bring me the file, please."

"Right away, sir," said Kahlil and turned toward the door. "Will you take lunch in your chambers, sir?" he asked.

"Yes, I would like a plate of hummus and some unsweetened lemonade, please," he said.

"General Aziz is fifty kilometers south of the city, inspecting an intelligence office and said he would be back to meet with you about two

PM this afternoon if that is acceptable," said Kahlil.

"Yes, yes," mumbled the Ayatollah and mused more about the trip.

Chapter 13

As predicted, General Aziz appeared shortly after two PM and was shown into the Ayatollah's chambers by an aide.

"Ah, General, good of you to come so quickly. Please have a seat and tell the aide if you want some tea or juice."

General Aziz was fiftyish, stocky and dark, his grey hair highlighting even more his dark complexion. His eyes were so dark brown that they appeared black in the dimly lit chambers of the Ayatollah.

"When we visit the facility near Qom, I want to have enough time to talk with Dr. Abeshami about his estimates of future capabilities, Ari. How long will we stay there on the present schedule?"

"Two hours, Sir," said Aziz. Do you want me to build in more time with him?"

"Yes, two hours is not enough. Arrange for three hours, please and tell him and his aides that we expect a full briefing."

"Very well, sir," said Aziz and sat down on the sofa facing the sofa on which the Grand Ayatollah sat. The table between them now had two nice-sized platters of hummus and pita bread slices and various garnishes. The Grand Ayatollah nursed his lemonade as they talked.

"The plan to separate our nuclear facilities and bury most of them seems to have been a good arrangement. Only once have we been attacked with any effectiveness and, thanks to the dedicated work of Dr. Abeshami's staff and the indentured servants, the damage was repaired more quickly than I had expected. I do believe, however, that we must press forward because our enemies must clearly be planning to hit us again, since the last strike did not disable us for long. The longer our negotiators can keep them tied up at the bargaining table, the better for our program. I just want to come back from this trip with a clear idea of how long it will be before we have actionable capability. The political part of the equation must always be considered as well as the production situation.

"Yes, Grand Ayatollah. The political situation is in a state of moderate flux just now. With a new mayor of Tehran who is just as militantly opposed to the pigs surrounding Jerusalem as his predecessor, we can count on his unwavering support. However, he is new enough to the office that we must wait a while to judge how effective he can be at convincing his people that we must destroy the Zionist entity."

"What occupies my thoughts just now is 'What will happen to our country if we strike first with a nuclear weapon and destroy the Zionist pigs. Will America, which has assumed a much less belligerent posture under the previous President, change course and become the feared foe it once was?'"

General Aziz pondered for a bit, while he enjoyed a large swipe of hummus on a piece of pita bread. As he finished swallowing it, he said, "As you well know, we have consistently misjudged the Americans. We thought that Reagan, for example would be a reckless cowboy and would conduct many strikes at our periphery, but he did not. When our Hezbollah associates bombed the Marine Barracks and the French embassy in 1984, we assumed that the Americans would strike back with a vengeance, but, instead, they withdrew and only conducted a local naval bombardment from the Battleship New Jersey as they left. I remember it well. We had our men deeply dug in and expected a swift and violent reprisal. Their latest President was a weakling, much more concerned with righting what he perceived as economic injustices and social programs than he was with foreign affairs. His posture was weak, as demonstrated by his insistent withdrawal from Afghanistan and Iraq. His withdrawal left the defenders weak and relatively defenseless and our people, who had waited patiently, were able to scoop up a wealth of military hardware and reclaim large areas abandoned by the Americans. Never in my wildest dreams did I believe the Americans would give us such a strategic advantage. This new American President Thompson, has his work cut out for him to retrieve the situation and get it back to where it was eight years ago, if, indeed, he can. I think the previous President has given us an advantage that will inure to our benefit for several decades to come. The real strategic issue for our leadership is to determine if the near future is the time to act or to wait for perhaps an even more advantageous time."

"Thank you, General Aziz. As usual, your analysis parallels my own and it is good to hear that someone in your position sees the situation as I and many of our leaders do."

"You told me when you elevated me to Commander of the Revolutionary Guard that you expected me to tell you what I thought as a military man and that I had your confidence and should say exactly what I thought. That is a wonderful instruction to a military man, sir, and I am most grateful."

Chapter 14

Yakob put his key into the big padlock on the revetment door. It was crusty with corrosion, but he used the little red tube on the can of aerosol lubricant to give it a shot of oil and, with a few wiggles, it yielded. Since he was in charge of all the aircraft in the squadron, no one thought it odd that he took a jeep and went up to the north row of revetments with a clip board, looking like he was making a regular periodic inspection.

Inside the air, which had mostly not been disturbed, smelled of rubber and jet fuel. According to the log, it had been three months since anyone had been in the hangar. He brought the work platform on wheels over next to the cockpit and mounted it. When he was up to the height of the cockpit, he used a tool to trip the latch to open the canopy. Hydraulic cylinders lifted it open. He climbed in and spent a moment generally surveying the instruments and levers, then the got out his pen and tape measure and began to make measurements. The distance of the throw of each control was measured and written down for later analysis. He reasoned he could put a control cylinder on one of the rudder pedals and control the rudder, another for the forward and backward movement of the stick and another for the side to side movement of the stick. Another would be needed for the throttle and another for the landing gear lever. Fuel tanks could be switched, if necessary with a solenoid at that control. If the stick solenoids could be anchored far enough away, the deflection of the controls would be minimally affected by the off center angle if both needed to be operated in coordination. The contemplated flight would be one way, anyway. No need to give any thought to creature comforts for a pilot, either. The altimeter could be replaced with one that sent telemetry to the base unit and the flight controller which encompassed the functions of the directional gyro and the attitude indicator would be a new one from a different aircraft, which would send its signals to the base, too. A power gauge with telemetry capabilities would be needed, too. All in all, Yakob spent more than an hour in the cockpit. When he climbed out, he had several pages of notes and measurements. He hesitated as he climbed out onto the work platform and looked back into the cockpit to think about anything he might have missed. Sensing that he had enough to keep him quite busy for a while, he resolved to return after the first mock-up to check for any oversights. It was so hot in the revetment that he was soaked with sweat. A few minutes in the dry air outside would dry that, though. He reversed his path and put the platform back against the wall and took his clip board and went out the door he had come in. The brightness of the noonday Mediterranean sun was startling, even for an experienced hand. The steering wheel of the jeep was so hot he could not keep his hands on it, so he used a rag looped around one of the spokes to steer as he started back to his office, a mile or so away.

With the seat removed, he could use the attach points to secure the guidance units that would be necessary. There were plenty enough attachment points and he designed mounts to use the one already available on the cockpit floor. He decided that he would rig an additional antenna for the guidance systems in case something went wrong with the aircraft antenna that was jutting from the fuselage behind the cockpit. A separate auxiliary stand- by battery was rigged in, too, just in case. The aircraft had a decent sized battery and would leave with a new, but thoroughly checked and charged battery. Things were shaping up.

As he returned to his office, he booted up his computer and began looking through his inventory of equipment. In the avionics list, he found a control unit for a Predator Drone.

"Wow," he thought. "I wonder how that got forgotten and left there."

He quickly paged over to the operations manual for the Predator. It was still in the hard drive, so he scanned over to the part that contained its physical specifications. There, he found the height, weight and measurements of the control unit, including a picture of it. The picture revealed only a metal box with numerous rivets in each panel, but it was clearly small enough to fit in the cockpit of the Mirage. The travel of the controls that attached to the various controls of the airframe were there, too, and he made notes. Just as a precaution, he copied the manual onto a compact disc for later use on his laptop or other computer.

Later, as he sat at his desk, between telephone conversations with his area subordinates who called in with activity reports and requests for supplies, he calculated the sizes and ratios of the bell cranks he would need to reduce or increase the travel of the controls of the drone unit.

Some controls were operated hydraulically and others were geared with bi-directional motors and long control tubes with gear toothed plates welded on. Clearly the unit would do everything he needed it to do.

He lifted the telephone and dialed a number he retrieved from his notebook. When the voice on the other end answered, he simply said, "Tell Falcon that Goshawk would like to have lunch tomorrow at noon." The reply was, "Yes, sir. Thanks. Good day."

Chapter 15

When Yakob walked over to the Mess Hall
the next day, late in the morning, he carried a
brief case with drawings to show General
Haim. He noticed the familiar Buick sedan
that General Haim used when he wished to
travel incognito in the parking lot. Yakob went
through the line and filled a tray with lunch
food and wandered back to the rear of the
dining hall. As he approached the back table,
a door opened just far enough for him to see
the familiar face of General Haim. He quickly
stepped in and General Haim closed and
latched the door behind him. It was a smallish
room, but had a central table and comfortable
chairs. General Haim had had an orderly
fetch him a lunch tray and the two men sat on
opposite sides of the table. Haim smiled and
asked Yakob to give the blessing, which he
did, in Hebrew. Then the two men began to
eat.

"Did you find something of interest, Yakob?"
asked the General.

"Yes, I measured the Mirage cockpit and
controls and I found a Predator Drone control
unit in our warehouse that seems to have

been forgotten. I checked on it, and I did not move or touch it in its wooden crate, but it is really there, in a dark corner of the avionics warehouse. I determined that the control throws are within limits and with a couple of bell cranks, I can fit it to operate the controls of the Mirage."

"That is excellent news, Yakob. What is your next step?"

"I need to find a forward looking television camera, so we can navigate visually when we close on the target. It may take a bit of searching, but if I cannot find one in our military inventory, I will rig one from a commercial source. Most military hardware of that nature is adapted commercial equipment, anyway."

"Assuming you can find the hardware you need, how long do you think it will take to up-fit the Mirage and be ready to go?" asked Haim.

"Since I am working alone for security reasons, I would estimate that this will take two or three weeks, working at night and when I can sneak away to the revetment," said Yakob.

"This is very good, Yakob. I think our ordnance people will have the explosive package ready in about the same time," said Haim.

"When we leave, I will give you a ride back to your hangar. If no one is there, we will pull the Buick inside and I will help you unload some new tires and tubes for the Mirage that I acquired recently."

After they finished eating and put the trays aside, Yakob showed General Haim the print outs of the pictures of the control unit and reviewed his measurements of the Mirage cockpit. He showed General Haim a photo he had taken of the interior of the Mirage and pointed out the attach points he intended to use for the control unit.

"Since we have a nice shop here in this hangar, I will be able to make the mounts for the control unit here and attach them to the unit at the revetment. With battery operated drills and grinders, I will be able to do this without using noisy equipment in the revetment, too."

"All this is taking place nicely, Yakob. I am very grateful for your work and dedication."

"It is an honor to be involved, General," said Yakob as the they put their materials back into Yakob's brief case.

General Haim went out the door by himself and left the dining hall without creating a stir. Yakob waited a few minutes and left also. When Yakob went out into the blinding sunlight, he noticed Haim at the wheel of his Buick. He already had the air conditioning going and Yakob got in and they motored over to the hangar.

Chapter 16

Lero was in his office on the north corner of the base. He was trying to decide how to achieve what the President wanted him to do.

"If we need to be in place up north, like in Natanz, how long would it take to get in place?" he thought. "If we need to be in Beshehr, it could be so much easier, but what about if the strike is to be somewhere south like Bandar Abbas?"

"Would it be better to get 'in country' well in advance, perhaps with the ability to travel, or just thrust in near the last moment and do what is required and get out?"

"How much advance warning will we have?"

"How can we smuggle in the laser designator?"

All these occupied Lero as he thought about tactics. He remembered when he was 'in country' before and was twice captured. No fingerprints were taken. His photo was not taken, so the SAVAK probably did not have his prints or photo on record. If he and Jean went in, masquerading as an industry representative trying to sell aircraft avionics to the Iranians, perhaps they could sneak components of the laser designator with the other aircraft radios and assemble it once they were near in time to needing it.

Another consideration was the effective range of the laser designator. With a fully charged battery pack, the designator could function at full power for forty minutes. Extra rechargeable batteries could be carried to multiply that time, though. The range, in clear air is a thousand meters, about three quarters of a mile, but the farther the target, the less precise the designation or the spot where the bomb or missile would seek.

He made a note on the check list to include a battery charger that could operate on Iranian power. Most countries other than the United States used two hundred thirty volts and fifty cycles per second of alternating current, so the proper adapter was necessary. Both Iraq and Iran used the same electric standards so the right adapter would work in both countries. Most Asian and Middle eastern countries used similar standards, too.

Transport was going to be a neat trick, too. If he were going to Besher, he could use a

Naval vessel and a night insertion to go ashore. If he needed to be in Tehran, it was quite another problem. Out in the country, like in Natanz or Qom, the logistic challenge would be more likely distance than infiltration or secrecy.

The ringing of his cell phone drew his attention away from his study of the map of Iran. It was Jean.

"If you will come over, I have something to show you," she said.

Teasing, he said, "Is it something you have showed me before?"

"No, silly, this is business," she feigned annoyance at his reference to a more personal matter.

"I found something that you might want to use on the next project," she said.

"I can come now, if that would be convenient," he said.

"Sure, come on," she said.

"OK, 'bye," he said.

The avionics shop was a half mile from the old Quonset hut that Jefe had chosen as the home office of the group. Lero was grateful for a car port next to the hut, so his car and those of the others who worked at and visited his hut could be sheltered from the desert sun.

Quonset huts came in different sizes and this one was about a hundred feet long and about forty feet wide, plenty of space for their purposes. To the outside, it looked like any other sun baked metal building, many of which sat in disuse since the shrinkage of the base from its peak years in the 1960s. This one had been nicely up-fitted inside for modern comfortable offices. Carpet and air conditioning and modern electric service.

He started the Grand Cherokee and went south down the road. Like many things there, the sun had baked the asphalt road and the sand which had blown across it for many years had turned it into a gray color just a shade darker than the surrounding sand of the base. The desiccating effect of the wind and the heat was ideal, though, for the storage of aircraft. With protective plastic wrap and plugs, an aircraft could sit there for years without deteriorating.

A long line of mothballed B-52s stretched out beside the road. He reached the Avionics shop in a minute and left the Cherokee with the windows open and went inside.

Jean was working in the shop behind the office. Because the shop was secure, he had to use his key to enter. She had an interesting looking item on the bench in front of her as he stepped in.

"What have we here?" he asked as she looked up.

"This, my dear, is a hand held laser designator, fresh from its manufacturer in Ohio. Jefe authorized me to order it a month ago and it arrived earlier by courier.

"Tell me about it," he asked.

"It is called the Rattler and has all the features we would need for your current project. Plenty of power, good range, light weight, good concealability, and we can partially dismantle it for quick reassembly and put it in one or more items of luggage or shop satchels. Its most qualifying feature is that it is the same as the one our friends have. I want to dismantle it and build the components into three of the avionics that we will be taking

95

with us to install. I can put it back together in a couple of minutes, once I retrieve them."

"How far, in clear weather, could we rely on it to paint a target?" he asked.

"The manual says the clear weather range is a fifteen hundred meters," she said.

"With the battery pack, we could carry a spare, which weighs less than a pound. Actually, the battery is the heaviest component of the whole thing."

"Can you test it to see if it lives up to expectations?" he asked.

"Sure, I can, but it will take two of us, one operating the designator and the other operating the sensing device. I would suggest that we do this ourselves to keep all knowledge of this system and the fact that we have it as close as possible," she said.

"Do you want me to operate the designator or the sensor?" he asked.

"You should operate the designator. I will operate the sensor. We can do this in daylight or after dark. These streets are deserted enough during the day and after dark that we can use our cars, too, so there will be less chance of being observed," she said.

"At, say, six hundred yards, how big a spot will the designator light up?" he asked.

"Let me look," she said, and after looking said "The manual says that at that range the designated area will have a diameter of about six inches. It is only visible if one is in direct line with the designator, or watching it splash over a target with special glasses, but the sensors will pick it up and evaluate the strength of the signal."

"Wow," he said. "Really good."

"We can take it for a try after lunch," she said.

"OK," he said. "Where would you like to eat?"

They were standing on opposite sides of the work bench, which was chest high and about twenty inches across, with a beige micarta top. She came around to his side and took hold of his shirt between buttons, and pulled herself up close and looked up at him.

"You know, this one of the few remaining places around here where we have not made love. I feel a strong desire to take care of that if you can spare the time," she whispered. "There are no surveillance cameras on just now, and I am the only one working today."

He looked at her upturned face and a wave went through him.

"Let me check the door," he said. There were no windows in the shop and as he checked the door, he turned off the overhead lights. The room took on a much more intimate ambiance with the lights out and the only light coming from a lit magnifying glass on the side bench. As he turned, he could see that she had unbuttoned her blouse and was pulling her skirt up over her beautiful thighs. As he watched in grateful amazement, she shed her outer garments as he walked to her.

He arrived just in time to help her with her underclothes. My, she was a beautiful woman. She helped him with his shirt and belt as he kicked off his shoes and kicked them toward the wall. He had not seen her pull the pillows from the sofa on the back wall while he was walking toward the door and light switch.

Just as he finished undressing, she pulled him down onto the cushions and made sure that their first encounter in the shop was very memorable.

Chapter 17

They had lunch at the Sub-Way and, with the tinted windows and the outside glare, no one could see them fondling each other as they ate. They felt like teenagers. He was glad she had not put her underwear back on.

After lunch, they returned to the shop and gathered up the designator and the sensing equipment and took them out to their cars. He took the designator in the Jeep and she took the sensing equipment in her Subaru Forester.

"If we go to the north perimeter road, we can measure off six hundred yards with the range finder and then we can test the designator. I will call you on my cell phone and we can keep line open as we work," she said.

"The only thing I don't like about your plan is that I cannot touch you when you are way over there," he said.

She smiled and gave him a squeeze and a very thorough kiss to hold him until she could get back closer.

He marveled at how beautiful she was and how gracefully she moved as she walked to her car.

In a couple of minutes, she pulled over to the side of the road, still facing away from him. His range finder showed that she was still about fifty yards short of six hundred, so when she called, he asked her to move forward about that amount.

Once the range looked good, he said, "Tell me when your sensing equipment is ready and I will shoot a sighter."

She put the phone down and plugged the sensor's components together. She said to him, "I have the sensor ready. The leaf parabolic antenna is about ten inches across, so this should be a good test," she said.

Lero pulled the designator over to the front seat and aimed it at her car, using the cross hairs in the telescopic sight attached to its top. He turned the unit on and, when it showed a green LED indicating it was ready, he pressed the red button to shoot a pulse of energy at Jean's car.

"Wow," she said. "Even though you were low by about a foot, I could see the laser light through my protective glasses. I am satisfied that the designator is powerful enough and you just barely missed hitting the ten inch antenna with your first attempt. Clearly this is more than accurate enough to do what you plan for it."

"Good," he said. "I will follow you back to the shop."

Once they had the two pieces of equipment back on the bench, they checked them over once more and then locked them in a steel cabinet on the south wall.

As he turned to go, she asked, "How is the planning going? Is there any kind of a timetable or a geographic clue yet?"

"No information yet. I think the time will be within the next sixty days, but the geographic consideration will be a last minute thing. That is why we have to plan for several contingencies. If we get better information, we can narrow the geographic plans a bit."

She walked him to the shop door. As he put his hand on the latch, she put her hand on his arm.

"Thank you for the pre-lunch celebration. I can still feel a tingle," she said.

He bent close to her and kissed her softly on the neck and then looked at her directly.

"It was unforgettable. I am so grateful for you, Jean. You are my dear woman."

They could not resist a goodbye kiss, which lasted long enough to be quite distracting.

"I can hardly wait to be alone with you at home," he said.

"Me, too. See you then," she said.

Chapter 18

"Lieutenant, I want you to arrange a passport for Barbara Weintraub, only using the name her brother uses – Hatzor. How long will it take your people to produce and "age" such a passport," asked General Haim.

"We will need a few days, General. If you need it done at emergency speed, I could probably bring it to you in the morning," said Lieutenant Seigermann.

"No, it is not an emergency. Normal course of business, but do alert me when you have it and I will meet with you. Thank you and, by the way, thank the guys who work for you in the encryption bureau. Perhaps it would be better if I come there to pick it up."

"The men and women in our bureau would be very honored to have you visit, General. It always boosts morale to have a visit from leadership. I will call you when it is ready."

"Thank you. See you later," said Haim and hung up.

In due time, the passport was prepared and picked up by General Haim. He had a nice visit with the encryption bureau personnel and thanked them for their loyal service.

"Working in a windowless basement room all the time must be cheerless," he thought as he left. "Thank you Lord for these people."

He used his special key to send the elevator back up to the lobby. His faithful Buick was waiting for him.

Once again, Haim met with Lieutenant Barbara Weintruab in Room 222 in Hangar 6 on the base. He arranged the meeting at two in the afternoon, so they would have a couple of hours without interruption.

At the appointed time, she tapped at the door and he said, "Come in."

Weintraub came in and shut the door. She came to attention and saluted General Haim. He rose and returned her salute and told her to be at ease and motioned her to a stool on the opposite side of the drafting table. He pulled the cover off of a map of Iran. He said, "Our plan is for you to fly commercially to Tehran on an IranAir flight from Athens. You may communicate with your brother by letter to tell him that you expect to arrive on a certain date for an extended visit. Tell him only to notify you only if the visit is inconvenient. If he asks how long, tell him a couple of months."

"That should be no problem, sir. The last time I talked with him, he was anxious for me to visit. I have not seen his youngest child."

"Once you arrive, I want you to spend a few days just visiting, but being aware of anyone following you or observing you on behalf of the government. Once you are satisfied that you are not being observed, you will dial a certain number on your cell phone and send a test message, in digital code, indicating this. After that, you will be contacted to give you a time and place to meet with someone who will give you the equipment you will use and an itinerary for you and your brother to follow. Your cover will be that you and your brother are traveling to visit relatives and we will supply you with names and addresses in case they check them."

"I understand, so far, sir," she said.

"Your contact will supply you with a laser designator and other appropriate supplies. There will be a thermite charge in the designator to enable you to destroy it if you and it are in danger of being discovered. As you know, you must not stay near the device once your arm the thermite, to avoid serious burns. You will also be issued weapons and emergency food and the other appropriate gear. A vehicle will be provided, too. It will not be new, but will be thoroughly checked out beforehand and will have some special features to help protect you and your brother and will have some special communications gear installed. As I earlier told you, your mission is to paint a target with the laser designator at the appropriate time. The target may be a building or a vehicle and may be moving, or, on the other hand, we may not be able to put you in a position to do all this and you will finish your visit and return home. If, on the other hand, we are successful, there will be extensive investigations and it will be prudent to remain with your brother in a very low profile until we determine that it is safe for you to return."

Weintraub said, "Your man from the special operations unit gave me a very thorough orientation on the laser designator. He and I used it several times at different distances and different times of the day, so I am comfortable with it."

"Good," said Haim. "Here is the passport the encryption bureau made for you. Leave your regular passport with Major Dev when you go. He will have money and travel materials for you and will arrange for you to go to London as Barbara Weintraub and, a few days later, to depart for Athens as Barbara Hatzor using this passport. You may be directed to travel to as distantly-separated areas as Rasht to the north or Bandar Abbas to the south. Our target will be traveling under heavy security, so this is the manner we have decided to use. As you paint the target with the laser designator, a very swift aircraft will strike the spot you designate. Be prepared for a massive explosion. Take care to protect yourself. If you are within two hundred yards, you will be in grave danger. If we are successful, do not flee the area, but hunker down and stay several days until our people advise it is safe to leave. Do you have any questions of me?"

"Not now, General Haim, but may I ask Major Dev if I have questions?"

"I would prefer, for his protection, that you call me at this number with any questions. This telephone number is answered constantly and the person there will be able to contact me quickly. Please feel free to call at any time," he said. "Your code name is Osprey. Mine is Falcon."

"Three days after you arrive in Tehran, take a walk around the neighborhood where your brother lives. Wear the green scarf that will be packed in your suitcase. A woman you do not know will pass in front of you and will drop a garment when you and she are in a position where no one can observe either of you. In the pocket of the garment will be a key and directions to a cache where your equipment will be. Wear gloves when you visit the cache, go in the heat of the day, and remove all the gear and take it with you. Take your brother with you to help you load the gear and do not return to the cache. I am sure your coaches have told you to assume that you are being observed or followed wherever you go, so take particular precautions. Once you have picked up the equipment, you will receive travel instructions by digital text message on your cell phone. Be careful to input the proper four digit code to unlock the cell phone. If another number is input, the phone will lock up, delete all information and become inert. If that happens, we will know it and we will arrange to get you a new phone. This is the last time I plan to meet with you before you leave. Please let me express my gratitude. I will pray for your safety every day. Good luck and may God bless you."

They stood. She looked him straight in the eye, came to attention, and saluted. He returned her salute and she left the room.

Chapter 19

Jefe and Alita stood behind the glass of the terminal at the Air Base. It was two AM and they had arrived just a few minutes earlier. Their baggage was on a cart, ready to be taken out to the aircraft. In the western distance, they could see the landing lights of a large aircraft. It disappeared behind some adjacent buildings as it made its short final approach.

In a minute or so, the plane taxied around the buildings on the taxiway and approached the terminal. The huge aircraft, a C-17, came to a halt on the tarmac in front of the terminal. Ground personnel opened the doors on the side of the aircraft and pushed up stairs so passengers could deplane and new arrivals could board.

A steward from the aircraft walked into the terminal and approached them.

"Ah, Mister Brubaker (Harry Brubaker was Jefe's "travel name," when he needed to give a name. He carried a U.S. Passport in that name) and ma'am, you will be seated in the forward passenger compartment. I will take your luggage to be loaded in the luggage compartment. We will only be on the ground for a short while, so you may board right away."

(Note to the detail inclined: Harry Brubaker was the Korean War fighter pilot, played by William Holden in the movie "The Bridges at Toko Ri, from the book by James Michener. Any pilot can tell you about that movie.)

Looking at his name tag, Jefe replied, "Thank you, Sergeant Candalesia, we will board quickly."

Jefe took Alita's arm and led her to the huge aircraft. The steward at the door directed them to the front passenger compartment. They passed through a bulkhead at the front of the cargo compartment and entered the passenger area. It was outfitted much like a modern airliner, with very nice seats because the distances covered by this plane were lengthy.

As they took seats on the right side, their steward approached.

"Good evening. I am Sergeant Coolidge and I and these other persons will be your crew on this flight. We will be departing soon, so please buckle up. We will be conducting a standard safety briefing in a few minutes as we taxi out to the runway. We will bring around some blankets and pillows for your overnight comfort and we will serve a nice breakfast in about five hours. If you need food or drink or anything else in the meantime, just push the call button above your seats."

Alita said, "Thank you, Sergeant Coolidge. We appreciate the ride. When will we arrive?"

"Our flight plan calls for arrival at Incerlik, Turkey in approximately ten hours."

"Thanks," she said and she and Jefe got settled in for a long night flight.

There were about twenty passengers in military dress and half that many in civilian clothes in the compartment. All seemed to be ready to settle down and sleep once the flight got underway.

In just a few minutes, the great plane started its engines and began to roll. It taxied out to the active runway in the dark of night, its huge landing lights turning the runway ahead to a shade of very light gray.

Obviously the pilots had acquired takeoff clearance by the time they got to the runway, because they did not hesitate at the threshold, but taxied onto the runway, achieved the center line and advanced the throttles to the stops. The huge plane rumbled forward and in twelve seconds vaulted into the desert night.

"Air Force 716777, fly runway heading, contact Approach on one two five decimal two. Have a good flight."

"Roger, tower, seven seven seven over to approach. Good evening."

"Approach, seven seven seven is off runway one two at Davis Monthan, squawking three three seven five."

"Seven seven seven, you are in radar contact. Turn to heading of zero eight zero and climb to flight level two four zero, expect three three zero in ten minutes. Join J-104 to Saint Simon, rest of R-NAV flight plan approved as filed."

(Note: J-104 means Jet Airway J-104. These high altitude electronics routes are for transport aircraft and business jets which fly at altitudes above eighteen thousand feet above mean sea level. RNAV means area navigation using the VOR system which has more than a thousand navigation radios on the ground in the United States. As soon as Seven Seven Seven passes over the San Simon VOR, it will be free to navigate by RNAV, or in this case, by GPS, on its flight path. Because this is a "quiet flight," the pilots will not be expected to contact Air Traffic Control after this hand off and will not be contacted by Air Traffic Control unless necessary to avoid traffic or for severe weather advisories.)

"Roger, approach, seven seven seven is turning left to zero eight zero and climbing to two four zero."

It was as quiet as in a modern airliner where Jefe and Alita sat. The lights of Phoenix, sixty miles away to the left rear were not within their sight. Jefe leaned his seat back   and positioned a pillow so he and Alita could snooze close together.

Ahead, in the flight deck, Major Secord and Captain Miles had already set the navigation radios on the VORs that strung out ahead to the east coast before they took off.   Then Miles input the identifier for Incirlik, Turkey, LTAG, in the Garmin 635 GPS Navigation

System. It had taken several minutes to enter all the numbers and once set, Captain Miles switched the flight director to fly to those VORs serially and compared the GPS flight path with the path provided for the VORs. The altitude was set on the flight director to flight level three three zero and he and Major Secord watched the dark ahead for the lights of Albuquerque. Even though it was over a hundred miles away, its lights showed in the distance, off to the left.

"Want a cup of coffee?" Miles asked.

"Sure, that would be fine," said Secord.

Miles pressed a button above him and in a few seconds, the flight deck door opened.

Airman Grayce Preston asked, "Can I bring you something?"

"Coffee for both of us, please," said Secord. "Cream and sugar. Thanks."

"Will do," she said and turned to fetch it.

"Those people we stopped to pick up at Tucson must be pretty important, diverting our flight like they did to pick them up. I wonder what they are doing?" asked Miles.

"Unusual things happen at Davis Monthan and Area Fifty One. No use being curious. They will never tell us," said Secord.

"Right," said Miles. There was a long period while neither spoke as the dark carpet of desert unfurled beneath them.

Chapter 20

The telephone rang in the office of the Commandant of CENTCOM in Tampa.

"General Frist's office. Major Gaines speaking."

"Major Gaines, this is Lero. L – E –R -O. I need to position myself on business on a carrier in the Persian Gulf sometime in the next two weeks. I am currently in Tucson. Will you please ask General Frist if he could approve my transport to Incirlik. I will be traveling with a woman companion and we will need transport to Athens from Incirlik, sometime within the following ten days."

"Right, Lero. Give me a secure number where I can call you back. The General will need to order some arrangements and we will get back to you."

"Thanks, Major Gaines. Have a good day."
He hung up.

Now things were beginning to line up. First he needed to get a flight to Tel Aviv for the visit with General Haim that the President wanted him to make, then to another place in the area to await transport to the ship. He wondered where to go to wait. Perhaps Jean would prefer to wait in Rome where she could shop and tour as they waited. If Lero finished his visit with General Haim and returned to Rome to wait for the right time, Jean could enjoy the area. Besides, the food in Rome was superb. He would need to call General Haim to give him a time envelope when he would like to meet, since General Haim had a busy schedule, too and might be traveling.

He dialed another number.

"General Haim's office, Lieutenant Levy speaking."

"This is Lero, calling from my office. I will be in your area in the next week and would like an appointment to visit with General Haim. Also, I would like his advice about transport to his whereabouts when he wants to visit. I could arrive by aircraft, or if he would prefer, I could drive down from Ben Gurion Airport. The best date for me is the fourteenth of the month."

"Thank you, Lero. The General is out now, but when he returns, I will ask him. May we call you at the usual number?"

"Yes, you can call me on the usual number. Thanks. Have a good day."

"Good day, sir," said Levy and they hung up.

Chapter 21

Yakob carried a large cardboard box from his workshop over to his car, which he had pulled into the hangar. He took his toolbox and flashlights and opened the door to leave. After he pulled the car out of the hangar, he carefully returned and closed and locked the hangar door. The revetment on the north end of the base was only about two miles by road. He did not have to pass through any check points to get there and since he had the only key to the revetment, as operations officer, he was confident that he could start work on the control package and leave his work partially completed to resume another time.

Once he was in the darkened revetment, he took the cardboard box out of the trunk and carried it over to the stair steps beside the Mirage. The lip of the cockpit was about ten feet off of the floor and he lugged the package up to the top platform of the movable stair steps. The whole package weighed about eighty pounds and he was sweaty after he lugged it up the stairs. He sat one last time in the pilot's seat and opened the lunch box he had brought. While he enjoyed his pastrami and Swiss cheese on rye sandwich, he pondered about the control package he was about to install. He had made two bell cranks, one to increase the movement of a control and one to decrease the throw of another. Both were of 6061T6 aircraft aluminum and the dim glow of the light on the aluminum outlined them both as they lay on the floor of the Mirage.

He knew what he was doing was important. It was important enough to General Haim, the Chief of Staff of the Israeli Defense Forces, that he would risk his job, his reputation and his pension on this project. Because Yakob was helping General Haim voluntarily and not "on orders" he would suffer the same or worse. Yakob felt the same slow burning rage that the General felt, though. This was a special chance to do something really meaningful and precisely retaliatory. What drove Haim, drove Yakob, too. Ari had been Yakob's childhood friend. They had gone through school together and even went to the same University. Ari left a wife and small children. This needed to be done.

After eating his sandwich and drinking the bottle of Gatorade that he had brought, Yakob got up and reversed his positon, putting his knees on the seat, so he could remove the mounting bolts with his ratcheting wrench.

There were four cross bolts, AN5 size, meaning that they were five sixteenths of an inch in diameter, and specially hardened. With the bolts out, the seat was loose except for the electric connections to the ejection features. Once he removed the threaded ring holding the two pieces of the connector together, he could get the seat out. He went out onto the movable ladder platform and went down to the revetment floor where he rolled a light duty crane on rubber tires over to the Mirage. It was an old World War II style crane, bulky, but strong and could be cranked by hand. He raised the boom enough to clear the cockpit opening and give enough clearance to swing the pilot's seat out. He cranked out enough cable to connect to the seat back and went up the stairs again. In a minute or two, he had connected the cable hook to the loop welded onto the back of the seat. Once he made sure that the seat would swing free, he went out again and down the stairs.

He eased the seat out, cranking slowly, waiting for the seat to clear the components of the cockpit that were on either sidewall. The seat came out easily. He cranked it up till it was clear of the side of the cockpit, then locked the crank and pulled the crane away from the Mirage's fuselage. He lowered the seat to the floor of the revetment over in the corner and returned the crane to its position, with the boom returned to its original position.

It was time now to return to his duty station and resume his activities as operations officer of Ovda Air Base. He backed the car out of the revetment, locked the door and motored back down the road to his hangar office. It was three o'clock, local time.

Chapter 22

"Sergeant Grimes, the telephone is for you," said Airman Fleet.

"Sure thing," said Sergeant Hamilton Grimes as he ambled over to the table in the hangar to answer it.

"Sergeant Grimes," he said.

"Ham, this is Tori Haim. How are you doing?"

"Tori, my goodness, I have not heard from you in a couple of years. Are you OK?"

"I am fine, Ham, but I need your talents for a project. Can you spare some time in the next couple of weeks?"

"Sure can. Is it anything interesting?" he asked.

"Yes, I think you will find it very interesting. No travel. Minimal risk and technically very up to date."

"Can you talk about it on the phone?" asked Grimes.

"No. I will send a Sergeant Sabah to meet with you and he will explain what we need and make all the arrangements."

"When may I expect him?" asked Grimes.

"I would expect he will contact you by telephone tomorrow afternoon, your time."

"Sounds good, Tori. I would really like to see you again. We had some good times together."

"I will be around for a visit soon, Ham. I appreciate your doing this for us. If you need to use any of your guys to help, please caution them about secrecy. If your superior officers get involved, tell them that you are working for Group 47 and to contact IDF Headquarters. That should get you clear of any trouble. Sabah will have an envelope with instructions and come currency for you and your men."

"Tori, you always take good care of us. I will get on it right away. Thanks again."

"You are welcome, Ham. We need you. We are so grateful for you. See you soon, I hope."

"Thank you my good friend. See you soon," said Ham.

Sergeant Grimes returned to his duties as chief ordnance man for the IDF Air Base at Tyre, Isreal..

Sure enough, the next afternoon about four, Grimes was summoned to another phone call.

"Sergeant Grimes, this is Sergeant Sabah."

"Been expecting your call, Sabah," said Grimes. "Do you have a package for me?"

"Yes, I would like to bring it by your hangar, it that is OK. Is your area secure?"

"Yes, the only men here with me have security clearances and will be working with me on the project. When will you arrive?"

"We have your hangar in sight. We will pull up with a truck in a couple of minutes. Please open the doors and stand by to close them behind us."

"OK, see you then," said Grimes and hung up.

In a minute or two, a six by six military truck with Star of David markings pulled up to the hangar. Airman Beyer had the door open and closed it promptly behind the truck after it entered. The driver cut the engine promptly to prevent a lot of diesel exhaust in the hangar.

Sabah got out of the passenger side and came forward to greet Grimes.

"Good to meet you," said Ham and extended a hand to shake.

"Got a room with a table?" asked Sabah.

"Sure, follow me."

The room adjacent to Grimes' office had a nice sized table where they could spread out their papers and things.

Good light and plenty of room.

"What have you got for me, Sabah?" asked Grimes.

"In the truck are the forward and rear sections of guidance gear for your one thousand pound dumb bombs. There are enough sections to rig up two bombs. There are instructions in this package. It should not be difficult for your technicians and you to put these together in a short time. When you are ready for them to be picked up, call me at this number (handing him a card) and we will pick them up. We estimate that it will take you about fifty man hours to do this. We will hang around on a TDY pass for a couple of days to take them back. Call me at this cell number when you are ready to have them picked up. By the way, how long have you known Tori?"

"I have known Tori since we served in the Golan Heights during the Hezbollah uprising of 1992. I was wounded and spent a long time in hospital. Tori visited me almost every day. After I recovered, I was posted to Aircraft Maintenance. Tory visits me often when he is up here."

"He spoke highly of you, Grimes. You must be good at your job."

"Tori is generous with his praise, Sabah. We go back a long way. I was a pall bearer at his wife's funeral."

"I remember the funeral, too. I saw you and the other pall bearers, but did not know who you were. Thanks for being good to Tori. He deserves it."

"I will call you when we are ready. My men should have the crates unloaded by now. We can let you guys out."

"Good. See you in a couple of days."

They walked out to view the crates and Grimes signed the letter for Sabah, acknowledging receipt of the crates, by number.

With the doors shut, in the dimmer light of the hangar, Grimes and Beyer carefully opened the crates. They were a bit surprised to see the components of the SPICE system that they had only heard whispers about. They carefully put the tops back on the crates to await delivery of the two bombs they were to up-fit.

Chapter 23

Major Nicholas Warshovski watched through the port window as the aircraft approached Patuxent River Naval Air Station. It was a bright moonlit night and from Flight Level Three Six Zero, he could see over sixty miles easily. The river estuary below was frozen over except for a small channel in the middle. A blanket of snow added to the brilliance of the tapestry below. His first officer, Captain Walter Weems was watching the DME wind down. It was set on the NHK VOR at Pax River, as they all called it. The DME, which reported line of sight distance to a navigation radio on the ground would only wind down to approximately seven nautical miles as they passed over.

Even though they were on a "silent" flight plan and did not need to report to anyone after they were turned loose by Dallas Fort Worth Center, and had not spoken to anyone in over three hours, Major Warshovski keyed his mike with the button on the yoke and spoke: "Pax River Approach, Military 407322, passing over your station."

"Roger, 407322, do you require any service?" said the airman manning the frequency.

"Negative, I used to be billeted at Pax River as a Marine Test Pilot and just wanted to say hello."

"Glad to hear it, three two two, for your information, Pax River reports temp at negative two, pressure is two niner niner seven. Have a good flight."

"Roger, Pax River. Best regards."

By the time that brief courtesy call ended, Warshovski could see the Atlantic Coast ahead. It would be a nice quiet night of aviating.

Sixty feet behind Warshovski, Jefe and Alita slept in adjoining seats, sharing one of the extra pillows the steward brought them. Their faces were only about three inches apart, a position they were very accustomed to.

As they slept, Jefe dreamed of a time before he was "Jefe" and before he was "Harry Brubaker." It was his senior year in High School, shortly before the homecoming football game. He was studying in his room when his mother called him from downstairs to come to the phone. Alita was calling to say that she had been elected an attendant to the Homecoming Queen and to ask if he would escort her onto the field at half time. She explained that her boyfriend, Scotty, who was a year older and had gone to Hampden Sydney, has asked her to ask him to do it.

"Sure," he said. "Just let me know what I need to do. Thanks."

The homecoming game was a high scoring slam bang type of game. Their team won by a touchdown after a night long see saw battle. He had walked her out onto the field at half time and back to their seats and all went well. They enjoyed the game with their friends. When he parked the Plymouth in her driveway, she got herself out and came halfway around to take his arm to walk to the door. She was not yet completely confident in her high heels on the hard surface. They chatted as he walked her to the door. She took out her key and opened the door. She opened the door and let is swing wide open. The darkened hall way inside led back to the kitchen where a dim light outlined the doorway. She reached around the door jamb and flipped the switch of the blinding overhead light and the porch went from extremely white to black dark in an instant. She turned toward him. He thought she was going to say "Thanks" for escorting him, but instead, she put her right hand over his left shoulder and drew him toward her. She turned up to him, drawing his face close to hers. He could see her dark eyes clearly. She slowly closed them and kissed him ardently. He was surprised in the max, but returned her kiss. He had never been kissed like that before. Her mouth was pursed slightly open. He could feel her tongue flick into and out of his mouth. It awakened something he had not experienced before. Long seconds passed. With her other arm, she had reached around his waist and pulled herself against him as hard as she could. They stood there together in the dark. When she let up and released him from her hug, she simply backed away, looking him directly in the eyes and shut the door. He had walked unsteadily back to the car.

His dream ended as the C-17 went "feet wet" over the coast.

Hours later, perhaps it was a bump of light turbulence, that diverted him from sound sleep to dream again.

Now it was several years later, Harry had finished a tour in the Air Force and returned to Bradford. He found a job in the intelligence branch of the government at the base east of town and bought a split level home on the south side of town.

By chance, he had bumped into her at the grocery store. She filled him in on her situation and he did the same. Turns out, her marriage to Scotty had not gone well. He drifted into alcoholism and they had divorced the year before. Harry asked her to dinner and they started seeing each other. He worked long hours at the base as a civilian contractor and she had a busy job as the Director of Personnel at the biggest hospital in town.

Then Harry was offered a position in Washington at the "home office." Leaving Alita and Bradford was a major item and was difficult for them both. She could not leave her job and he wanted to pursue his career, too, so he left and they began seeing each other much less. In time, she had met George and decided to marry him. Telling Harry in a letter was very difficult for them both, but it seemed to be the right thing to do.

A year and a half later, Harry had met them both together at a Church Ice Cream social. It had been very painful for Harry to see her so happy with George, even though, deep down, he wanted her to be happy. Long years passed.

Chapter 24

"General Haim's office, Major Avner speaking."

"Major Avner, this is Jefe. I would like to call on General Haim next Wednesday afternoon. Would you see if it is convenient and call me back?"

"Yes, sir. Give me the number, please."

Jefe repeated the satellite phone number and thanked Major Avner."

"You are welcome, sir. Talk to you later."

In about an hour, Jefe's satellite phone rang.

"Hello," was all Jefe said.

"Sir, could you arrive about two PM on Wednesday at the Army Headquarters in Jerusalem?"

"Yes, that is fine with me. See you then. Thank you."

Both parties hung up. Jefe put the satellite phone back in its lead sheet lined case and turned to watch Alita sweep into the room in the new negligee she had bought that day in Rome.

"What do you think?" she asked, stepping into the rays of the late afternoon sun in the parlor of their suite.

"I think the negligee is beautiful and that you are the most exciting woman in the world. I also think I had better get a shower to be presentable for the rest of the evening."

"May I assist you with your shower?" she asked, teasingly.

"A shower is so lonely without you, dear. Of course I need your help to be completely clean."

Much later that evening, they went down to the hotel's restaurant for an elegant dinner.

Over the table, she asked: "When will you leave? When will you be back?"

"I will leave tomorrow morning and will be back Thursday afternoon on the El Al flight. I will get a cab to the hotel and we can have a late dinner."

"Seriously," she said, taking his fingers in her grasp over the table, "I am very grateful to be included in your travels. I hope I do not slow you down or make things more complicated. This is just wonderful. I have never been to Rome before. I appreciate coming along so much."

"It seems so natural to have you with me wherever I go, dear. I wish I could take you with me, tomorrow, but this is a sensitive matter and I need to move quickly. I hope you understand. I will take you to meet my friend sometime soon."

"You know if you are gone overnight, you will have things to catch up on when you get back."

"I promise to give that my undivided attention," he said as the sommelier poured them another glass of Beaujolais.

Chapter 25

Lero was ushered into the secure office of General Haim. It had been two months and a few days since Ari's death. Haim hugged Lero like the good old friend that he had become. General Haim still had the dark and sunken look of someone who was suffering in grief. The first thing the General said to Lero was how deeply touched he and family were to have him and Jefe and the President come to the funeral.

After Lero took a seat across from General Haim, the General spoke:

"I know it was a serious security risk and it meant a lot to our people. After you left, I told our security personnel and the friends assembled that we had had a very private visit from the President of the United States and other dear friends."

They both paused for a while.

"Mr. Murfree told me to tell you that our people have concluded that the attack in

Netanya was orchestrated by Hezbollah and paid for by the leadership in Iran."

"Thank you, Lero. It is always good to have your country's confirmation of our suspicions," said General Haim.

"He also told me to tell you privately that if you need any additional technical assistance in regard to the investigation, he will put our facilities at your disposal."

"Tell Mr. Murfree he has our gratitude. Tell him also for me personally that I greatly appreciate his coming to the funeral. Ari would have been so honored. Your Mr. Murfree took quite a chance doing that. It meant a lot to me and to the family. We will always be grateful. Now is there anything that he needs that I can provide?"

"Not just now, Sir. He just wanted me to touch base with you and assure you of our sympathies and our concern over the continued terrorist activities of Hezbollah and the Mullahs in Tehran."

"Yes, well, they continue to be a serious problem. We continue to step up our efforts to counter them. It consumes a lot of our time and treasure, but we view it as an existential threat. Will you be returning to your country directly?"

"No, sir, Mr. Murfree wants me to consult with another leader in this area. He told me to assure you that if we learn anything material, he will make it available to you."

As they rose to end the visit, General Haim walked Lero to the door of his office suite.

When they shook hands, General Haim's eyes had a peculiar look. He was moved because Mr. Murfree had sent his most trusted spokesman, personally, to call on him.

"Tell Mr. Murfree that I treasure his friendship and will always be grateful for his attendance at the funeral."

"I will do that, sir. Also, my friend, Jean, asked that I tell you that she prays for you constantly."

"Tell your friend that I am touched by her generous heart."

They parted with a handshake and Lero turned to walk down the long hall and out into the scorching summer sun of Jerusalem.

He rode the afternoon El Al flight to Rome.

Chapter 26

Jean asked Lero to come to her shop when it was convenient. Remembering the spectacular earlier visit, he was able to tear himself away from his report writing that afternoon to visit her shop.

"I had an idea about your present research," she said. "I know that you need to get into Iran and to be somewhat mobile and you also need to take the laser designator with you."

"That's right," he said. "I have been trying to come up with a scheme or an infiltration mode to let me or us do that. What is your idea?"

"How about if I partially dismantle the designator and insert those parts, separately, into normal aircraft avionics. I can reassemble them when we need them. Since we know that the French are dealing with the Iranians in aircraft replacement and maintenance parts, why don't we pretend to be avionics technicians from one of those companies and gain entry into Iran that way? Once we are "in" we or you can go where you or we need to, to fulfill the rest of the mission. Since I

144

don't speak French and you do, you can tell them that I am your Algerian assistant and mistress. Being such misogynists, the Iranians will love that. Having a woman along may allay any suspicions about you, too. They will think your off duty time would be occupied by amorous pursuits with me. I could dress in Algerian head dress and look the part. Because we will need to travel to several air bases to check and possibly replace navigation and autopilots in military aircraft, we can ask in advance for permission to travel about the country. We could even get a local asset to be our driver."

"Jean, that is positively brilliant. Thank you so much. I was having such a time thinking of a pretext to get us 'in country.' I will ask Jefe and Mr. Murfree what they think and let you know."

It was two o'clock, local time.

Jean put her hand on his on the bench. She said, "I remember what a nice visit we had when you came last time, but it was much too short. Can you take more time this time? I want to be sure that we aren't so rushed."

"I will lock the door," he said as he turned away.

Chapter 27

It was not unusual for General Haim to pay a visit to the Kidon group of Mossad, but the names on the doors only reflected that the offices were billeted to the Israeli Defense Forces. He knew all of the senior officers on a first name basis since he and other top officers had chosen them and approved their promotions when appropriate.

The second office on left belonged to Major Dev Hatzor. Thirty years old and at the top of his game, Hatzor was in charge of the international or Caesarea branch commando unit. Each man and woman in the unit had special qualifications in addition to their commando training which was roughly equivalent to the American seal training program. These special men and women had personal experience with the language and culture of foreign countries. Many had lived in foreign countries and traveled extensively. They were well trained and efficient killers. Almost all of them had lost someone close and dear to them to one of the nations or groups that were constantly harassing Israel and wished for its destruction.

The door to Major Hatzor's office was open and Haim stepped in. Hatzor recognized him immediately and jumped to his feet and came to attention.

"At ease, Dev, you will get a hernia jerking to your feet so quickly," said Haim with a smile. Hatzor relaxed, and smiled at Haim's attempt at humor.

"What brings you to my humble office today, General?" asked Hatzor.

"I need you to pick two men for me for a sensitive mission. They must both be familiar with Disneyland and have traveled there some. I will need one to be familiar with cities in roughly the northern half of the country and another to be familiar with the south. The mission involves reconnoitering and electronic surveillance of a particular event. I would prefer to brief your candidates personally and exclude you. If this mission goes awry, I do not want you to have any personal repercussions."

"General, there is no need to be so protective of me. Any of us here would do whatever we could to help you. We all owe you so much."

"You are most kind, Dev, but I want to isolate you so you will not be harmed. Once you have picked your candidates, give me a call and we can schedule the briefing. I will need them to be detached for ninety days, at least."

"I can get back to you right away, sir. Can you stay for lunch? The men love to see you in the mess hall. There is nothing better for morale than to see that you respect them enough to visit and eat with them."

"I would be honored, Dev. Your men are the heartbeat of our forces."

They walked the two hundred yards to the mess hall in the bleaching brightness of the noonday sun.

Chapter 28

The next day, Dev called General Haim's office. When General Haim came to the phone, Dev simply said: "Candidate One will meet you in Hangar 6 at three PM local time if that is OK. Will be wearing a New York Yankees ball cap and dressed in civvies. The second candidate will meet you at four PM, if that is OK. Will be wearing a dark blue jogging suit.."

General Haim simply said, "Alright. Thank you."

The next day General Haim parked his Buick next to Hangar 6. He left his cover (hat) on the front seat and strode into the hangar. The hangar was busy with numerous mechanics pulling maintenance on fighter jets and a helicopter. He strode around, nodding to the workers and smiling. About half way across the hangar, he spotted the Yankees ball cap and approached.

As he walked up, she tried to conceal her astonishment at who was addressing her.

"Who sent you?" asked General Haim.

"Dev sent me," was the coded answer.

"Wait here a couple of minutes, then come to room 222."

She nodded without speaking, still deftly concealing her surprise.

He walked up a flight of stairs and went into Room 222. While she was delaying following him, he looked out over the air base from one floor above ground. It always pleasantly surprised him to see how much better one could observe from one story above ground.

He had just turned around when she came through the door and closed it quietly behind her.

"Pardon my surprise, General Haim. Major Hatzor did not say whom I was to meet. I assumed it would be a Major or Colonel.

"It's all right. Please be at ease. Tell me your name."

"I am Lieutenant Barbara Weintraub."

General Haim extended his hand to shake hands with her.

Then, he motioned for her to sit.

"I am a bit surprised to meet you, Lieutenant. I have to say, I honestly did not expect Dev to choose a woman. Please do not take that as a chauvinist remark. I have no such conscious bias. Did he tell you what the mission might entail?"

"Only that it would involve travel and electronic surveillance in a foreign country and might last for as long as ninety days."

"For his protection, that is all I told him."

She nodded as if she understood.

"I want you to undertake a very delicate mission for me. Only three people know what I am about to outline for you. If you choose not to undertake the mission, which I will quite readily understand, there will be no negative reflection on you and no report will go into your file. However, if you decline, you must be my guest for the next ninety days or so, until the mission is completed or abandoned. Do you want me to continue?"

"Yes, sir," she said quietly.

"We hope to hit a target in Iran in the next ninety days. You will have to infiltrate and subsist there and may have to travel several hundred miles while you are 'in country.' The reason I was surprised that Dev picked you is that you will be infiltrating Iran and they have very strict rules about women being unaccompanied by a male family member when out and about. Do you know why Dev picked you?"

"It may be because I have a brother in Iran, sir. My father married an Iranian woman when he was stationed at the Embassy in Tehran in the mid-seventies, while the Shah was still in power. She was killed by a member of Savak after the Ayatollah Khomeini came to power in1979, for having defiled herself by having married an Israeli and borne children by him. I was five at the time. I learned to speak Farsi from my father."

(NOTE: Savak is an initialism which stands for Organization of National Security and Information, the secret police and oversight network of Iran.)

My father grieved terribly for several years, but later met and married my step-mother, who is an Israeli from Sidon. I was raised mostly in Sidon, but I have traveled to Iran many times to visit my brother and his family. He lives in Esfahan with his wife and children. He was wounded in the war with Iraq in 1982 and lost his right leg below the knee. Before that, Savak had him under constant surveillance, but due to his loyalty to Iran in the war and because he is a handicapped person, they have left him alone for several years. He can travel with me and be my guardian. Do I have to tell him what this is about?"

"I would rather you only tell him that you are conducting a very sensitive electronic surveillance mission. Are you confident in him, Barbara?" asked Haim, looking directly at her, but with a friendly gaze.

"I know he despises what the Mullahs have done to Iran. Before the war and before Khomeini, he planned to study in the west. He wanted to be an architect and help rebuild Iran. I would trust him with my life."

"I regret to say it, but you will be doing exactly that if you involve him in this project," said Haim.

"Can you give me a general idea of what you require on this mission, sir?" she asked.

"Basically, we want you to be in a position to train a laser designator on a certain building or vehicle at a certain time, then ex-filtrate without detection.

"How close to the target must I get, sir?"

"Fifteen hundred meters at the farthest, but about a fourth of that would be ideal."

"Is the target a facility or a person, sir?"

"A person."

"I would assume that if you are going to all this fuss, the target is somewhat important," she said.

"You could say that," said General Haim.

"There will be a counterpart to you in the southern regions of Iran at the same time you are 'in country.' You will not know his identity and he will not know yours, but you may communicate, if necessary using code names and messages. All these details will be given to you and you will be briefed further as we get closer to the date. You should not discuss this with anyone. If anyone attempts to discuss this with you, other than your commanding officer or myself, call me immediately on this number," he said, handing her his card.

"Thank you for undertaking this mission, Lieutenant. We will be in touch."

"Thank you for your confidence in me, sir," she said as she stood. They looked at each other for a moment. Then she saluted and turned and left the room.

When she had gone, General Haim again turned to the windows and prayed, "Thank you, Lord for Lieutenant Barbara Weintraub. Keep her safe, please."

"Where do we get such people?" he asked himself as he turned and made for the door.

Chapter 29

Later that afternoon, General Haim was sitting in a folding metal chair in a far, dark corner of the hangar. The place was deserted since the previous shift had finished their maintenance work. Lieutenant Beri David (pronounced Barry Dah-veed) stepped into the four foot gap between the large hangar doors. He paused once inside to let his eyes adjust to the lower light. He then stepped forward between the aircraft looking for his contact. He had only been told that an officer wished to speak with him about a covert mission.

General Haim's chair made a metallic sound as he rose from it and stepped forward a bit. David heard that and headed toward the sound. He could see the man walking toward him, but did not recognize his rank until he was just ten feet away. He tried to conceal his surprise, but failed. He came to attention and saluted General Haim. General Haim returned the salute and told David to be at ease.

Haim led David back to a table near a window in the back wall of the hangar. He motioned for him to sit and took a chair opposite.

"Who sent you to see me?" he asked.

Beri said: "Dev sent me."

What did Major Hatzor tell you about this meeting?" asked Haim.

David said: "He said a commando was being sought for a delicate mission 'in country,' sir. He did not tell me that I would be meeting with the Chief of Staff. You can imagine my surprise."

"I remember being a Lieutenant like you, Beri. I was sent to deliver a satchel of dispatches to the Chief of Staff once myself. I remember what it felt like, but please be at ease. I just need to talk to you to find out some things about you and decide if you are the proper person for the mission. Please do not be offended if I do not choose you. I am confident that you possess the skills and training for the mission, but I need particular qualifications in this instance. Whether you are chosen or not, you must never reveal that we talked about this. Do you understand?"

"Yes, sir. I understand," said Beri.

"Dev would have chosen you carefully, but I need to know if you have any particular skills in avionics."

"Before I was chosen for the Special Forces, sir, that was my job. I was in the Avionics Department of the Air Forces and stationed at Tyre when I was selected for further training."

"Your dossier says that you speak Farsi. How did you come to acquire that skill?"

My father was a Military Attache in our embassy in the 1970s. I was raised with the local children and learned it by immersion. I went to a school for English speaking students, but I needed to learn Farsi to converse with the other children in our neighborhood. It is a sad commentary on people that I was accepted as one of them when I was a child of five, but by the time I became a teenager, they began to hold my Jewish faith against me and grew distant and derisive. By the time I was sixteen or so, I was clearly ostracized. Prejudice like that is clearly learned and not inborne in people, isn't it?"

"Yes, I am afraid it is," said Haim. "It is my firm belief that we Jews are the most despised among minorities. At the same time, we harbor no ill will against any group. It is only when we are attacked or maligned that we retaliate."

"Can you tell me a bit about what it is that you want me to do for you, sir?" he asked.

"Yes," said Haim. "First of all, you will be working directly for me. There are only a very few people who know about this mission and we want to keep it that way. If you decide not to undertake this mission, your record will not reflect any negative comments. This will not appear on your record. However, if you decide not to undertake the mission, you will be my guest until the mission is completed or abandoned."

"Tell me what it entails, sir," said Beri.

"I want you to infiltrate Iran and take a laser designator with you. At a certain time and place, I will want you to paint a particular target. After the strike, you will destroy the designator and slip out of the country and return. We will be waiting to help you ex-filtrate. You may be in country for as long as ninety days. Is there any reason why you should not accept the mission? Are there any personal matters that might dissuade you from accepting?"

Beri sat silently for some moments, then said, "No sir, there are no personal matters. I can accept the mission. When will you want me to act?"

"Thank you, Beri. Stay in your present billet with your current work assignment and we will contact you. Expect to hear from us again within two weeks."

The General stood and shook hands with Beri. Beri took the general's hand , then stepped back, came to attention and saluted. Haim came to attention and saluted in return. Then Beri turned and walked toward the gap in the hangar doors.

Haim was alone in the hangar again.

He waited until Beri had departed and five minutes later, he left the hangar and got in his Buick to return to his office.

Chapter 30

Lero caught up with Jefe at the Athens airport. They met in the bar on the observation deck where they could see across the airport with all the planes arriving and departing. As they sat across from each other at one of those tiny tables barely big enough for a plate of food, let alone two plates, Jefe leaned forward to say: "We have found an entrée that we think will work. One of our proprietaries is located here at the airport. A charter business, for all external, appearances, but we find out a lot at the airport. Our local guy Reger, overheard men from another company on the airport talking at lunch a couple of weeks ago. Seems that the Iranian Air Force is trying to find some American avionics to upgrade their F-4 Phantom II aircraft. These airplanes were manufactured in the seventies and sold to the Shah before he was deposed. With the embargo in place, they cannot purchase American avionics through normal channels, but an avionics business like the one located here on the airport, can find things on the used marked that are still a generation newer than the Iranians have. The Iranians want these flight directors delivered and installed in the Phantoms, which are deployed, or I would say, scattered all over Iran, from Tehran to Qom, Esfahan, Bushehr, and Bandar Abbas. We offered to deliver the radios and have a technician install them for a package price. One of the specifications is that they must come into the country in one shipment and the smaller the group involved, the better. The Iranians will pay one half up front, which includes the radios, travel money, money for installation, and incidentals. They expect to have the radios brought in to the Esfahan Airport, since it receives direct flights from Europe and three of the Phantoms you will need to work on are at Hesa Airport north of Esfahan. We have given them your photograph and a dossier that indicates that you are a French national and will be traveling with your Algerian assistant and girlfriend. You will be introduced as a retired French Air Force avionics technician who will be an independent contractor employed by the local business to bring the radios into Iran and install them and check them out. We figure you will be "in country" for about three weeks."

"How did you ever arrange for all this? How did you entice the Iranians?"

Jefe said, "As you know, sometimes it is best to hide in plain sight. We thought we would simply place an ad in Trade-A-Plane."

(Note, Trade-A-Plane is a commercial magazine published in Crossville, Tennessee. It contains feature ads and classified ads for virtually everything related to airplanes, including aircraft for sale and including aircraft radios, which are referred to as avionics.)

"We put an ad in the commercial/military section of the avionics ads for the new radios under their Manufacturer name and model number. We used the surplus shop at Davis Monthan and advertised that the radios were surplus. Most readers would not recognize these radios and navigation devices by these numbers, but our friends at Mandrakos Avionics spotted them right away and bought the whole lot. We had tapped into a stream of information indicating that they had previously done business with the Iranian Air Force. They put the deal together. We also advertised in the 'Technical Services' section of Trade-A-Plane that an avionics expert was available to service and install a number of radios by model number and manufacturer, and they went for it. Since the Iranians were so needy for new radios, and evidently were scouring all sources for them, they found the ad in Trade-A-Plane from Mandrakos and the other ad for the avionics technician the whole deal went together nicely. We simply waited and hoped they would notice and they did. They must have needed the services of an avionics technician to remove the old radios and install and test the new ones, someone who had experience at the manufacturer, because they had not had any one who knew enough about the American radios to install and test them. Then, we simply made up a dossier for you, showing that you had the appropriate background. Since anything French is for sale, we thought it best to make you a French national and naturally, being a red blooded Frenchman, you would need to take your girlfriend along. Jean is perfect for this role. She is beautiful enough to distract the Iranians and she is the best female marksman I have ever known, not to mention that she is a world class avionics technician. We only had to run the ad for two months before it caught the Iranians' eye. Because of sensitivities about sending Westerners on this kind of a mission, payment will be made from the Iranian embassy in Islamabad with a hand off. They will pass half of the money in advance and we will wait a discrete interval afterward to contact them with your travel itinerary. Once 'in country,' you will travel where they want you to go to service the planes. They estimate that it will take you at least three weeks, barring unforeseen complications. If the contract is fulfilled without the need for you to perform the laser maneuver, we will try to stall to let you stay there for a while, but if there is no need for you to stay longer, you and Jean can simply come out the way you go in, by commercial air. If the real reason for the trip occurs, we will have to become imaginative about your extraction."

"How soon will I need to be ready to infiltrate?" Lero asked.

"In a time envelope that opens on the thirteenth for five days," said Jefe.

"OK, I can be ready. Better brush up on my French. Jean is in Rome having a great time. We will be ready in time. How do we arrive?" asked Lero.

"You need to pick up the pallet of radios here at Mandrakos Avionic Systems, so you can fly commercial from Rome, but use the Passports that we will send you by courier to your hotel. The Iranians are to arrange air transport to Esfahan from here. You will travel in country by taxicab. We have arranged for one of our guys to be your driver. His name is

Zabol and we will give you codes to make sure that the driver you encounter is indeed Zabol. We will send you specs of the radios, too, so you and Jean can study up."

"OK," said Lero with a smile. The two men enjoyed their lunch and caught their planes. Jefe took the sea taxi and was back at the dock on Keros in time for Alita to pick him up in their ancient Hillman sedan. He treated her to a seaside fish dinner in town before they went to their villa.

Lero's flight landed at a little after eight Rome local time and Jean was waiting for him at the hotel. He called her from the airport to let her know to expect him.

Chapter 31

The next day, the desk called in mid-morning, to say that a courier had arrived with a package for him. Lero went down to the desk to meet the courier. The desk clerk pointed with his chin toward a youngish man in civvies as the military calls them. He had a brief case handcuffed to his left wrist. Lero motioned the young man toward an alcove in the lobby where they could converse rather privately.

"Lieutenant Mackinaw, sir. I have a envelope for you and I need you to sign for it. I also need to take your picture, in good light, for my report."

Lero held still while the young man took his picture with a smart phone. Then he opened his brief case and handed Lero a clip board with a receipt clipped to it. Lero noticed that the receipt had a time and place as well as the number on it that was scrawled on the envelope. They agreed on the time of day and he dated it, filled in the time, and signed it. Once Mackinaw had put it back in his brief case, he handed Lero a manila envelope about an inch thick.

Then Mackinaw said: "Thank you, sir. Do you need anything further from me?"

Lero said, "No, Lieutenant, thanks for bringing this. Good luck to you."

"Thank you, sir," said Mackinaw and turned to stride toward the lobby exit.

Lero waited until Mackinaw had disappeared, then rose and slowly walked to the lift, as they call them in much of the world outside of the United States. He noticed that no one in the lobby appeared to be paying any attention to him.

Back in the room with Jean, he got out a black plastic wand from his luggage and turned it on with the rocker switch on the end of its handle. He spent the next ten minutes sweeping the suite for bugs and cameras. Once he had done his scan, he took the envelope and put it on a table in the corner of the room, in front of the sheer curtains so as to have plenty of light.

Jean looked beautiful in a dark purple bath robe as she stood next to him while he opened the envelope. He could not resist fondling her. She repaid him with a juicy kiss on the neck. They decided to take a break and come back to the envelope and its contents later.

Once back in a disposition to concentrate on the envelope, he sat down at the table and drew out the entire contents and spread them on the table.

He took the inventory list and double checked to make sure that he had received all that was intended for him. The list checked. Six items.

The first item was a letter, on thick parchment like paper with the great seal of the Iranian Republican Guard. It was written in English, French and Arabic, one paragraph of each.

"This is to introduce Monsieur Daniel Roman, a French national, who is an avionics technician, contracted by The Islamic Republic to replace aging radios and other sensitive navigation devices in our aircraft at several airports in the Islamic Republic. His assistant, Madame Jeanne Bennettoire, an Algerian national, is also an avionics technician and will be accompanying Mr. Roman and assisting him in the replacement of these sensitive radios and navigation devices. Please accord Mr. Roman and

Mme. Bennettoire every courtesy at your disposal. You may refer any inquiries about this letter to the undersigned.

In the name of Allah and Mohammed, his Prophet, and the great Islamic Republic,

Yours truly,

General Ali Askari Hummadi
Chief of Staff"

There was a large seal with a half inch wide red ribbon through it below the signature. The letter was most impressive. The letterhead was impressed and had raised lettering and was quite ornate. Lero and Jean looked at it admiringly in the morning light.

There was a list of avionics with the numbers of each that would be shipped and specification brochures for each type. Lero and Jean could see that they needed some time to study those.

The Passports were in order and were stamped to show previous usage to travel from Paris to such places as Algiers,

Benghazi, Cairo, and Muscat, as well as vacation trips to Bern and Cannes.

Also in the packet were several discs with French conversational lessons that they could play on their laptop computer.

"I have never been a French girlfriend before. How will I know how to act?" Jean teased.

"You don't need any lessons in that, my dear," said Lero, with a knowing smile. Jean blushed and came over and sat in his lap as they put the first disc into the laptop. He slipped his arm around her waist to keep her from sliding off. The satin gown she was wearing could be slippery, and he did not want her to fall.

Chapter 32

Jefe had arranged for Zabol to pick up Lero and Jean at the Esfahan airport. They had flown in from Athens on a flight that arrived late in the afternoon. Lero was engrossed in getting their cases cleared from Customs so they could leave the airport when Zabol approached him.

(All conversations were in French.)

"Do you need local transport, sir?" he asked.

Lero replied with the code response. "Yes, we will need your assistance with these cases, too. There is a pallet of equipment that we will need to pick up at the freight terminal. But let's leave it there for now. The airport seems like a secure enough place. We can pick up the pallet later."

Zabol responded: "In that case, I will need to hire a truck and driver to pick them up. Are the contents delicate?"

"Yes," responded Lero. "The cases contain aircraft radios."

Satisfied that he had indeed encountered Dan Roman, Zabol said: "I will be back in a moment," and he went to get a cart.

Jean had been waiting in a sitting area nearby and when she saw Zabol approach Lero, she slowly walked up as Zabol left.

"Is he our driver?" she asked.

"Yes. His name is Zabol. He will be back in a minute. Just wait with me."

The Customs inspector finished looking at Lero's passport and Jean's and at the letter of introduction from the Air Force Chief of Staff's office identifying Lero as a French aircraft radio technician and identifying Jean as his Algerian companion and fellow technician. The inspector stamped the tag on each case to show that he had inspected them and dated and signed each one. Then, with a nod and tip of his hat, unsmilingly, he handed the Passport and other documents to Lero, ignoring Jean, as was the custom.

Zabol reappeared with a wheeled cart for the suit cases.

"My taxicab is at the door to the left. It is the brown Mercedes. I have left the air conditioning on and you may get in. I will bring your luggage and these cases for you."

"Thank you, Zabol," said Lero and turned to take Jean's arm to go to the taxicab.

After a few minutes, Zabol appeared with the luggage and cases and put them in the trunk of the taxicab. Then, he took his seat and motored away from the taxi stand toward the airport exit.

"Where to?" he asked.

"Let's leave the pallet until tomorrow. The Surjan Hotel, please," said Lero.

Zabol nodded but did not speak. After they had driven a distance south toward the center of town, Zabol pulled in to a market parking lot and put the taxicab in "Park."
He turned in his seat and said, "Better we confer here than at the hotel. I had the cab swept this morning and I am confident in the absence of sensing devices for the moment. I am confident that we will be followed because a person in your position always is. Jefe said you might need my services for a week or so. I am at your disposal. These cards have my cell telephone number on it."

Lero said: "Yes, we will need you for probably a week. We might have to travel long distances on short notice, so best to keep the fuel tank topped up. Just now, we need to get settled at the hotel and await instructions. Very unlikely we will need you again tonight, but plan on picking us up about ten tomorrow morning. We will need to go to Hesa Airport and will be there most of the day. You will not need to wait with us, but we will need to be picked up after about four PM local time, unless we call you with a change."

Zabol said: "Hesa Airport is about sixty kilometers from the hotel. Plan on an hour and a half to get there. I will be waiting at the taxi stand at ten tomorrow. I brought each of you a pistol. You will not be searched anywhere in town, but I don't know about the airport. You can be sure that your luggage will be searched while you are away from your hotel room. Leave nothing sensitive there."

He handed them each a loaded nine millimeter Glock Model 17, with an extra loaded magazine.

"Thanks, Zabol. Very thoughtful," said Lero.

When they arrived at the hotel, Zabol busied himself while Lero and Jean registered. The hotel was set back from the road about fifty yards and had a wide sweeping semi-circular driveway. There was a covered portico out front for cars to pull up into the shade. The lobby was open and had those overhead fans that seemed to be in all lobbies in this part of the world. Large potted palms decorated the spacious interior and there were several groups of large overstuffed leather chairs that reminded Lero and Jean of the old John Marshall Hotel in Richmond, Virginia.

Chapter 33

Using the telephone in the room, the next morning, Lero dialed the number he had been given to contact the Iranian authorities to tell them that he, his assistant and the radios were ready to get to work. The telephone was answered on the second ring. "Colonel Kozzum's, office, Sergeant Dakot speaking."

In Farsi, Lero said, "This is Monsieur Daniel Roman, reporting that I have arrived in Esfahan and we are ready to begin our work."

"One moment, please," said Dakot.

After a few seconds, a voice said, "This is Colonel Kozzum,   We are glad you had a safe trip. A driver will come to your hotel in two hours to take you to the Air Base where your first assignment is. He will have an itinerary for you to give you the next base and the number of aircraft and radios that are to be exchanged. If you have any questions, you can call us at the number you dialed. It is manned constantly. Thank you."

Lero said, "Very good, Colonel Kozzum, we will be ready."

True to his prediction, a black Land Cruiser pulled up to the hotel on time. The officer, Lieutenant Farrid, greeted them in French. He said that the air base was about an hour's drive, considering noonday traffic and asked if they were ready to go.

Lero replied that they needed to go to the freight terminal at the airport to pick up the pallet of radios. Zabol had arranged for a truck to pick up the pallet at the freight terminal and it was to meet them when he called to tell the truck driver to do so. It all went together nicely and the two cars arrived at the freight terminal just after the truck. The driver had backed his truck up to the loading dock at the terminal and the warehouse men had brought the pallet over to the edge of the dock. They all were just waiting for Lero to sign for the pallet and they could put it on the truck. Lero showed them his Daniel Roman French Passport and signed the form on the clip board for the warehouseman. In a few minutes, they were on their way to the Hesa Airport, north of Esfahan.

By the time they arrived, it was after two PM, local time. The Officer in the Land Cruiser stopped at the gate. He got out and showed the gate guards his papers and gestured to the second car and the truck. In a moment, the guard came to their car and took their Passports. He returned to his guard station and scanned them into the base computer system, then he returned them, saluted the Lieutenant and waved them through.

The hangar where the planes were kept that he and Jean were to work on was on the north west corner of the base, almost a mile from the front gate. The base appeared pretty secure, with a ten foot high chain link fence and camera towers every couple of hundred yards. In a few minutes, the group pulled up to the hangar.

A small military vehicle, similar to a Jeep, was sitting at the doorway of the hangar. The hangar doors were closed. The Sergeant in the Jeep saluted Lt. Farrid and unlocked the regular door beside the big hangar doors so they could go inside.

After talking with the Sergeant inside and making his own brief inspection of the hangar, Farrid returned outside and came over to the car. He said: "All arrangements have been made satisfactorily. You may work as long as you please today. Sergeant Farrid and his men will provide security for you. If you need something, they can contact their commander for assistance. They will stay with you until you leave. Thank you."

He turned and unlocked the hangar doors and, with the help of Farrid's men, rolled the massive doors open enough for the truck to pass into the hangar. Then, he went over to his Land Cruiser and left.

Lero, Jean and Zabol got out of their car and entered the hangar to begin their work. As they had requested, there was a small, portable crane to lift the aircraft seats out and lift the radios, too. The hangar contained four F-4 Phantom II aircraft. They helped Zabol and the driver unload the pallet of radios. There was a small lift truck for their use and the driver started it up and lifted the pallet off the truck and put it in a corner where they could access it to get the new radios off and put the old radios back on.

Chapter 34

Lero was lying on his back on a pad in the floor of the F-4 Phantom fighter. Jean was standing over him jimmying the new radio into position. Lero was working with a small Maglight flashlight in his mouth, both hands grasping the twenty pound radio from below. Jean had just plugged in the master coupling that connected the radio to the power source and to the instruments on the panel that would give the pilot the ability to set the radio and to observe its outputs to help control its flight. As Lero was looking up through the tangle of wires and tubes and Jean was looking down, they both heard a soft hum. Jean gave Lero a knowing glance and reached over to retrieve the testing set from its position on top of the panel. They both looked at the screen where an oscilloscope normally was fitted and saw a five inch square screen light up a soft green color. Then after about a minute, there was a string of two digit numbers displayed. Lero carefully copied the numbers onto a small note pad he kept in his pocket. It was a bit challenging to write while lying on his back, but he managed. There were five rows of numbers and he copied them all. Then he pushed the notebook up to Jean for her to double check his work. She found one error in the fourth line and made the change and said: "Looks good."

Lero retrieved the notebook and put it back into his pocket. After they had installed both of the radios in the Phantom, later in the afternoon, they did a full function check on the radios, which necessitated a normal circuit activation by turning on the master switch. Because the radios were electronic and digital, rather than the old kind where one could tell the frequency setting or the function setting on the dials, they had to have the tower alerted so that any signal generated would be understood to be coming from that aircraft and could be ignored. Because Captain Reza needed to communicate their request to the tower, they asked Zabol to tell the Captain that they needed to power up the Phantom's internal electrical system and to alert the tower. Reza then used his hand held radio to get approval from the control tower. In a minute, he nodded to Zabol, who said to Lero and Jean, "OK to power up."

Then Lero flipped the red master switch up to the "On" position. Dials and gauges immediately lit up all over the panel. He isolated them one at a time until only the flight director that they had installed was receiving power. Then he set the director to a certain frequency to see if it were receiving the glide slope. The indicator on the upper middle of the panel jumped to life and the vertical bar of the gauge moved quickly over to the right, indicating that the glide slope beam was to the right of the aircraft. The other outputs of the radio seemed to be operating fine, too.

Lero said to Jean: "This looks OK for now. Tell Zabol to tell Captain Reza that we will need to have this aircraft towed to the center line of Runway Three Zero to calibrate the localizer and the glide slope."

"OK," she said. "Whoever flies it for the first time will have to adjust the altitude read out to correspond with the altimeter and radar altimeter, too."

"Right," Lero said. "I doubt that they will let us do that, so we will have to tell the Wing Commander to have the pilots check and adjust the altitude readout. Let's wait until Captain Reza finds out when the Commander wants to do that before we decide whether to start the installation of the radios in the other plane."

They climbed out and went down the ladder, one at a time, then went over to where Zabol was standing and sat down in the folding chairs. It was after three o'clock local time and they had been working on this aircraft since about eight AM.

In a few minutes, Captain Reza came back from the Commander's office. He said, "No pilots are available until tomorrow morning. We can do the testing then."

"Alright," said Lero, "Let's remove what we can from the other plane and be ready to start again tomorrow morning."

They pulled the roll around ladder platform over to the other Phantom and opened the canopy. Next, he and Jean rolled a portable crane over next to the plane. They raised the boom above the cockpit.. Then they connected its hook to a harness that passed around the canopy and held it upright. They then disconnected the cockpit canopy from its hinges by removing the hinge pins. Then Jean went back down to the hangar floor and cranked the canopy up free of the aircraft. Then she rolled the crane over into a clear area and lowered the canopy onto a pad on the floor. She rolled the crane back over the plane for the next step. Lero was already inside the cockpit and, using a ratcheting wrench, removed the four bolts holding the seat to the rails on the aluminum floor of the cockpit. Typically, the seat could be rolled back and forth to adjust for the leg length of the individual pilot, so Lero removed the guard from the front and the back of the rails, then pushed the seat forward enough to lift the seat free of the rail in front, then repeated the process for the seat in the back. Once the electrical connectors for the ejection apparatus were unplugged, he told Jean that the seat was ready to be lifted out. She lowered the nylon rope and the hook by hand cranking. When Lero had secured the hook to the loop on the back of the seat, he gave Jean a hand signal to begin raising the seat. By guiding it with his hands, Lero got the seat to come up out of its position and hang from the nylon cord over the cockpit. He then climbed down and helped Jean roll the portable crane away from the plane. Then she cranked the seat down to the floor and she and Lero put it on a dolly to be rolled over away from the plane.

"That is enough for today," he said. "Let's go get some dinner and rest up for tomorrow. Zabol, ask the Captain if they would prefer that we take dinner in the mess hall or go into town for dinner."

Zabol went over to the Captain and asked.

In a few minutes, he returned and said that they could leave if they wanted to and come back tomorrow morning. They packed up their tools and got in Zabol's taxi for the ride back to the hotel. Tomorrow, they would go back to the airport to pick up the pallet with the radios and avionics.

After finishing the jobs at Hesa Air Base, they were told that their next assignment was at the Air Base at Bushehr. They left after dinner to drive at night because of the temperature and the need to drive more slowly with the trailer of radios. They had installed enough radios that they no longer needed a truck and had decided on a trailer to haul what was left.

Chapter 35

They had been driving for about three hours. They were about a hundred miles southwest of Esfahan on the road to Bushehr and Lero and Jean were asleep in the back seat. Unexpectedly, Zabol brought the car to a stop, seemingly in the middle of nowhere. Jean and Lero sat up to see a group of six men in the headlights, blocking the road. They were armed with Kalashnikovs and one had an RPG launcher. Zabol rolled down his window and asked the man who approached what he wanted, in Farsi. The man said to Zabol, "We want all your valuables. Throw them out onto the pavement, wallets, rings, watches, money, weapons." By this time, the six had arrayed themselves in a semi-circle in front of the car. Zabol translated for Lero and Jean. He then explained that his passengers were a Frenchman and his Algerian assistant, on their way to the air base at Bandar Abbas to change out old aircraft radios for new ones.

The leader said, essentially, he did not care who they were, "throw out your valuables." Then he noticed that Lero's assistant was a woman. He demanded that she get out of the car. Zabol protested in Farsi, but the leader brandished his weapon, so Zabol told Lero and Jean what the leader had demanded. They were very frightened but did not attempt to comply with the leader's demands. The leader pointed his assault rifle at Zabol directly and ordered him to get out and open the door for Jean to get out. Zabol told Lero and Jean what the leader had said and got out and came around to the passenger side rear door to let Jean out. Jean was dressed in a chador and was covered from head to foot and she got out of the car shakily and stood with Zabol. The leader demanded that Jean come and stand in the lights at the front of the car, which she slowly did.

"How do I know that she is not carrying a weapon?" the leader asked Zabol.

"She is a scientist and does not carry a weapon," said Zabol.

"Have her take off her chador," the leader said. (Note: Chador is the native costume of Iranian women, usually black or dark gray. It is a large semi-circular garment, worn over clothing or, rarely, just underclothes.)

"Sir, it is most objectionable," said Zabol. "This lady is not armed and your request is out of line."

"Tell her to take it off or I will have my men take it off of her," said the leader.

"She does not understand your language, sir," said Zabol. "Let me explain to her what you have asked."

"Be quick about it," said the leader, with growing irritation.

Jean shook her head and sobbed when Zabol told her what the leader was demanding. Zabol pointed at the leader's assault rifle and told Jean she must comply.

She was really crying by now and all the thugs were leering at her. She was terrified, but began to unfasten her chador. Just as she let it drop to the pavement, now standing in her underwear in the headlights, the leader stepped forward and reached for her. His hand stopped short of touching her because there was a loud noise and the back of this head sprayed out blood and brain tissue over the road. He collapsed in a heap. No one had seen Lero open his door and put one foot on the road. In a flash, Lero raised himself with one foot on the door sill and sprayed the remaining five men with nine millimeter rounds. Three were killed instantly and two were wounded and fell to the pavement. He ran to them and kicked their weapons away from them. Zabol came over with his pistol he had retrieved from the car door pocket and held the surviving men at gun point. Lero went over to Jean who was in shock, standing still in the headlights in her underwear. She was looking at the bleeding leader lying at her feet in the road and seemingly could not take her eyes off of him. His eyes were locked open. There was a neat hole in his forehead just above his left eye. Lero hugged her and held her a while, then he knelt and retrieved her chador from the road and helped her wrap herself in it again. Then he led her to the car and helped her in.

He went back to Zabol who was holding the survivors at gun point. One man was losing consciousness and had an obvious chest wound. The other man had a leg wound and was not in any real danger.

"Zabol, tell this man that we will let him live. Tell him that the others got what they deserved for disrespecting a woman, especially a guest in their country. I will gather up their weapons and drag the bodies out of the road and we can leave."

Lero opened the trunk and put the assault rifles and RPG in and then came back to Zabol and covered him while he got back into the driver's seat. Then he got in the back seat and Zabol motored away with them.

Jean was clearly very shaken up by whole episode. Lero got out a pint of brandy and gave her a healthy swig of it. She coughed a bit, but it helped her calm down. He took a gulp of it himself.

"Oh, God, I was so scared," she sobbed. "Hold me."

Lero said: "It's okay now. I love you," and he held her tight.

"Zabol, thank you for being so reliable. You were there for us and I will never forget that. Thank you."

"It was my honor, sir. I am so glad you had a weapon at the ready. If you had not, we would all probably be dead," he said quietly.

They motored on a while in silence, grateful to be putting distance between themselves and what had happened. In an hour, just as dawn broke, they crested a ridge and saw Bushehr below ahead of them.

Chapter 36

"Where would you recommend that we stay?" asked Lero.

"Let me stop near the center of town and I will catch another taxicab and go scout a good place for you both. I will leave the motor running, so you can have air conditioning. Do you want to stop and get something to eat and drink before I do that?" asked Zabol.

"That would be just fine," said Lero.

Eventually, Zabol parked the taxicab at the fringe of a large outdoor market and left them inside with the doors locked. He was gone about fifteen minutes. When he came back, he was carrying a basket and a newspaper. He got in the taxi and showed them the contents of the basket. He had three large melons that looked like cantaloupe, but were green with yellow areas. He had several bottles of water, including a gallon jug, and a bag full of sweet pastries. They gratefully and eagerly ate a good breakfast.

Lero said, "If you could get us some rooms with a view of the provincial capital it would be good. Get yourself a nice room, too, or we could share a suite if you would prefer. The schedule calls for us to be at the airbase at Bandar Abbas in three days, so we have some time to get organized. Can you arrange for secure storage of the taxicab until we need it or are ready to leave Bushehr? I can give you enough money for local taxicabs for you to look around."

"A city this size should have a good secure storage business. I will look around once we find a place to stay," said Zabol.

Zabol had been correct. The balcony of their room looked out onto a large square and the provincial capitol was just down the road half of a kilometer. He could see all the way down the shore line to the dome of the reactor about four miles away.

At about eleven AM local time, activity began to pick up on the street below. They were on the fourth floor and had a good view of the area nearby as well as over to the eastern edge of town, where the land began to slope up into low hills. They kept the doors opened, with the linen curtains blowing in the breeze. They noticed from within the room that a white Toyota SUV came by with men looking at the surrounding buildings. He noticed that they had several assault rifles, too.

His cell phone vibrated in his pocket. However, this message did not come in from the cell phone system, but from the satellite. All of the agents in the group had been equipped with special cell phones that received regular transmissions on the eight hundred fifty megahertz frequency that most cell phones use, but also received on a discreet frequency of approximately nineteen hundred forty five megahertz, which was conveniently tucked into the higher band reserved for the third and fourth generation smart phones. As a precaution, messages were transmitted in two digit pairs of numbers and could be decoded using the memory in the phone. Any attempt to use the phone by entering a pass word other than the correct one would disable the phone. There was also a feature that, if a special four digit number were entered, the phone would self-destruct in twenty seconds. This text message was a string of two digit pairs. He copied them down and consulted his code book. The coded message was: "Christmas eve. Rudolph is fifteen today. Big Mac. Top hat. One half click," which was also code, and the whole message was followed by a two digit number that was assigned to him. Without that number, the message was to be assumed to be a fake or a diversion of some kind and disregarded.

Chapter 37

It was just a little after four bells of the watch, two AM, local time. There was a soft tap on the bulkhead above his bunk. Lt. Beri David awakened and stirred. In a minute or so, he sat up on the edge of the bunk. The droning vibration of the engines hummed beneath his feet, permeating the whole boat.

It had been four days since he boarded the boat, under the cover of night, north of the Straits of Hormuz, but on the Iraqi side of the channel. The captain had adroitly brought the boat alongside the American frigate, Luther Burns. He had been ready and quickly climbed down the ladder to the deck of the fishing boat. The transfer took only a few minutes and the fishing boat pulled away toward the Iraqi side and on the port side of the Burns so any Iranian radar would not detect that the ships had met in the channel. For all appearances, the boat was an Iranian registered fishing boat with a crew of six, plying its trade in the Persian Gulf. The boat was fifty two feet long and sixteen feet wide at the widest. Beri donned the clothing offered to him by the crew, so he would blend in if they were boarded or scrutinized by an Iranian patrol boat.

The first afternoon, an Iranian Boghammer boat, purchased by the Iranians from the Danish Navy, pulled up as it approached from the starboard bow. The captain of the patrol boat waved to the fishing boat captain and asked in Farsi: "How is the fishing?"

The fishing boat captain responded "Pretty poor here. We will make our way north because other fishing boats report good catches up north of Karg Island."

"Good luck," said the Iranian. "Report any problems to us on the international frequency."

"Will do," said the fisherman, and the boats parted to go on their individual ways. Beri had been standing on the deck while this exchange took place. An Iranian sailor stood behind the heavy machine gun on the ship's deck, but made no aggressive moves, although he was obviously ready to act if needed.

Now, after three boring days of droning northward at a fishing boat pace, Lt. Rasheed had awakened him to begin preparations to infiltrate the Iranian coast. David began with a visit to the head, where after attending to his daily routine, he applied black face covering so his white face would not reflect any light in the crossing. He put on heavy long underwear and a wet suit. He retrieved his mask and flippers from beneath his bunk and went forward to rejoin Lt. Rasheed. Even though all crewmen spoke Farsi, they were all American soldiers or sailors, of Iranian extraction, who had volunteered for service on this fishing boat to be "eyes and ears" for the U.S. forces as they maintained vigilance up and down the Persian Gulf.

Rasheed told Beri that they lay six miles off the Iranian coast and that Rasheed was going to take him ashore in an inflatable boat with an outboard motor, then return to the fishing boat. Both Rasheed and the captain were going to use infrared flashlights to achieve rejoinder when he returned. Rasheed was from a village nearby and knew the coastline very well.

David had assembled a case of supplies, clothing, weapons and ammunition, communications devices including a portable transceiver and satellite phone, and the laser designator, and the all-important thermite charge to incinerate it all, in case of need. The captain and crew had only been told that David was going ashore to perform some electronic surveillance and that they might be needed to retrieve him at some date within the next sixty days.

The camouflaged case was covered in a vinyl covering that was to keep it dry and to conceal it with its black color.

On the deck, the deck hands brought out the inflatable boat and inflated it. Then they attached the outboard motor and lashed the two gas tanks to loops in the sides of the boat. Four of them lifted the assembled boat and lowered it over the side opposite the Iranian shore. Once it was stabilized on the surface, they put a ladder over the side and one of them went down to help load the boat. The black clad case was lowered to the sailor and he lashed it to a loop in the bow. Rasheed went next and assumed his position aft next to the motor. Then the sailor came up and David went down the ladder. Rasheed pulled the starting rope and the ten horsepower outboard came to life. In a minute they pulled away from the fishing boat and looped to the west and came around behind the boat and made for the shore. Rasheed kept the speed moderate to keep the sound down. He told David if they were hailed by an Iranian ship to heave the case overboard. It has been attached to a weight that would take it to the bottom, but which would be removed if they made it OK to the shore.

Long minutes passed. They were making about fifteen knots and it took about twenty minutes to make it to shore. As they got about a half a kilometer from the shore, Rasheed slowed and began looking for a good place to put ashore. Since they were all blacked out, they could approach the shore stealthily and choose the actual place of landing carefully.

It was a moonless night, overcast above and darker than average. They finally found a little cove between two good sized rock outcrops and put in there. It turned out to be the mouth of a small creek, about twenty feet wide. Rasheed navigated up the creek until the motor began to touch bottom and he turned toward the bank. In a foot and a half of water, he stopped and motioned to David to go ashore. David lowered himself over the side and, holding onto the boat with one arm, unfastened the case from the sinking weight and from the loops on the side of the boat.. He hefted the case and turned to go ashore. Luckily, the bottom was sandy, but firm and he walked out of the water steadily. When ashore, he turned to wave goodbye to Rasheed.

He picked up the case again and went up the bank into the scrub brush to find a place to open the cover of the case. He did so, and unwrapped the case. He rolled up the cover and put it inside the case, along with his mask, flippers, wet suit and gear. Then he dressed in the black well-worn clothes he had chosen earlier and put on the Greek boots he had brought. He retrieved his compass and GPS and his Browning Hi-Power nine millimeter handgun, put them in zippered pockets to keep from losing them. He also carried an Iranian Passport indicating that he lived in a suburb of Hesa, north of Esfahan. He put the wet suit, flippers and mask in the case and buried the case at the edge of a clearing, being careful to conceal the burial by smoothing the sandy soil over the hole. He created a waypoint on his GPS for the cache. With all of his gear transferred to an Iranian army surplus knapsack, he swung the sack onto his back and put his arm through the second strap. A woolen shepherd's cap completed his ensemble. The whole process had only taken eight minutes. He looked back down the creek and Rasheed was out of sight. He turned and started into the brush, looking for a place to hide and get ready to hike to the highway, which, according to his map, lay about a mile to the east.

Once he reached the road, as dawn was brightening the eastern sky, he turned north and walked along. Using the GPS and the map, he determined that he was about eighteen kilometers west of Borazjan. He determined to walk east toward the city and hopefully, to catch a bus from there northward. As he walked, he overtook a medium sized herd of goats being driven along the road and fell into step with them. The smell and the dust would discourage anyone from approaching him and he wrapped a scarf around his mouth and nose to help him tolerate the dust and the smell. He walked slowly all morning and reached Borazjan after noon. When they reached the edge of town, he broke off toward the right and took an alternate, but parallel path into the city. The dust and the smell of the goats was good cover for him. He stopped in a market and bought a melon and some bottled water. Somewhere upwind, he detected someone was cooking something that smelled appetizing, so he held the bag with the bottled water and melon and went toward the smell. The market was crowded at noontime. He soon found out where the good smells were coming from. A group of chador clad women were tending pots of stew that were bubbling over small kerosene heaters. The menu was simple, a paper bowl of stew and a plastic spoon. When he got to the head of the line, he said, in Farsi: "How much for one bowl?" The woman said "Fifty thousand rials." He reached into his pocket and offered her a bill. She stopped stirring long enough to make change, then scooped out a bowl for him and handed it to him, without expression or speaking. He accepted the bowl and spoon with a nod and turned away to find a place to sit down and enjoy his lunch. A low wall was a popular spot to sit and as he approached, two men got up and left, so he sat where they had been. He began eating the stew, little bites at first because it was so hot, but bigger bites as it cooled. Then he cut open the melon and ate it. He saved a bottle of water until he was finished.

As he left the spot on the wall, he walked past the oil drum where trash was burning and threw the bowl and spoon and melon rinds and the empty water bottle into the barrel. He started out of the market square toward the east, which he thought would lead him to a bus station. He asked a passing pedestrian where the bus station was and got directions, now changing direction toward the north. Within a half hour, he arrived at the bus station. He smiled when he saw an old Flxible bus from the forties and fifties. It was in pretty good shape for its age and it still had the old multi-piece R5 degree wheels and twenty inch tires. As luck would have it, his ticket to Esfahan assigned him to a much newer Mercedes bus and he was relieved to find that when he boarded, it did not smell too bad. He watched the old Flxible bus out of the bus' rear window until it was out of sight. The bus stopped at several towns on the way, but made it to Esfahan about eight the next morning. He grabbed his bag from the luggage door and made went looking for a big breakfast.

He did not have to go far. In the building next to the bus station, there was a restaurant that served both inside and outside. He took a seat at a table outside. A waiter appeared right away. Beri ordered feta cheese, Lavash bread, quince jam and sweet tea. Fortunately, the waiter brought him a whole loaf of bread and generous bowl of jam and feta cheese. He appreciated the delicate tastes and the combinations. The tea was excellent, too, much weaker than usual and the sweetener brought to the table was honey with part of the comb intact. It was a breakfast not to be soon forgotten. When he had eaten all he could, he kept the left over bread. There was no jam, feta or honey left over. The check was for Thirty thousand rials, about a dollar and a half. He gave the waiter three bills and tipped him with coins. The waiter smiled, showing several missing teeth, but with bright very dark brown eyes. Beri put the bread in his duffel and slung it over his shoulder and started north again. He walked around Esfahan most of the rest of the day, looking for a place to get a room. He finally settled on an old inn that had a balcony that ran the full length of the second floor and had a nice view. An elderly man was at the counter and Beri asked him if he had rooms available.

"Yes, indeed, sir, I have a few rooms. What would you require?" he asked. By now Beri began to wonder if any of the locals had a full set of teeth.

"A room for myself for a few days. Do you have any rooms on the second floor?" Beri asked.

 As was the custom, the innkeeper took a key from the board behind him and led Beri upstairs to a room. It was on the front of the building and had a balcony like he had admired from the street.

In response to the quizzical look of the innkeeper, Beri nodded and smiled and they went back down to make financial arrangements and get Beri a key.

Weary from all the travels, Beri took a warm shower in the bathroom at the end of the hall and then lay down for nap. When he awoke, it was well after dark, and ideal time for a little exploring. Because of security concerns, he took all of the sensitive things he had in his duffel bag with him.

After he had been walking for about half an hour, he came upon the local television station. He decided it would be a good place to make a report using his hand held transceiver. Usually, a man in his position would be using a satellite telephone, but he was not carrying one on this mission, and he knew that there was a repeater in Esfahan that would receive and relay his transmissions to a passing satellite, and he thought the stray radio signals would be less detectable near such a high powered radio frequency source. He sat on a low wall and took out the notes he had made in the room using the code book. A row of two digit numbers was lined up on the paper he held. In case of interception or loss of the code book, he was to include a final set of digits that indicated that all was well and that he was indeed the transmitter. He had not written these down on his list, but had memorized them   If the recipients of the message did not receive the last two digits on a message, they would assume that the code book had been intercepted and would be put on guard. He knew that his code book was unique to him and that no other agent had the same codes, so they would not need to warn others about their code books if his were compromised. He turned on his transceiver and transmitted the columns of digits. What he sent said: "In Esfahan. All OK. Waiting for messages." He turned off the transceiver and began his walk back to his rooming house.

Chapter 40

Beri David drove along in the night. The Land
Rover he had rented had a full tank of gas. It
was a beautiful moonlit night. At a point, he
turned off the headlights to see if he could
see well enough to drive without them. The
desert sand was bright enough in the
moonlight that he could see well. It reminded
him of the night, long ago, when he drove his
1956 Plymouth from Lynchburg to Durham on
such a night. Only on that night, the area was
covered with a cold ten inches of snow. He
had turned off the headlights and driven many
miles in the moonlight. That it came back to
him now was proof that that night was
unforgettable. Such beauty.

In time, his GPS indicated that he was closing
in with his target, so he slowed. He came to a
side road where the GPS indicated that the
target was about half a mile to the right, or
west, as he motored south. He turned onto
the sandy road and slowed again. The road
led slightly uphill and in about a quarter of a
mile, it crested a low ridge. On the other side,
he could see for quite a distance. There was
a building in the distance with outbuildings. It
turned out to be a deserted farmhouse, its

mud brick walls etched with the pockmarks of thousands of windy days.

The GPS indicated that the target was to the right, before the house. He got out of the car and took his military ditching tool and his musette bag with other tools in it. He walked about a hundred yards to a point where two old crumbling stone fences intersected. The GPS indicated he was at his target. Since the GPS could only sense within a sixteen foot circle where it was, he could not tell where his package was. He took out a key fob from an American automobile and pressed the unlock button. He heard a very slight chirp and moved toward it. When he thought he was standing over the spot from which the chirp came, he pushed the unlock button again. This time, he could tell he was within just a couple of feet of the chirp. He squatted down and pushed the button again. This time, the chirp was louder and seemed to be just behind him. He turned and put down the musette bag and flashlight and used the ditching tool to begin to dig. At a depth of about six inches, the tool hit a solid object. He used the red filter over the flashlight and shone it into the hole he had scooped out of the sandy dirt. The object was a khaki colored plastic case, about eight inches wide and ten inches deep and twelve inches long, about the size of a popular ammunition can. He quickly removed the case and filled the hole back up. He gathered his equipment and hurried back to the Rover. In ten minutes, he was back on the road, heading north, still with no headlights.

As he came to a small settlement comprising about a dozen houses and buildings, he pulled off the road next to a high wall and behind a large truck. He took out his flashlight, still using the red filter, and shone it on the case. He unsnapped the cover and opened the case. Inside were the components of the laser designator, three pieces of black composite, all held in place securely by foam specially cut for the components. He picked up each piece and looked at it to see how it would be connected to the other components. When assembled, it would be about ten inches long and weigh less than a pound and a half. Also in the case was a thermite charge to incinerate the designator and the case when he was through with it or to prevent its being captured. He replaced the components in the case, added the automobile key fob and snapped the cover back closed. Now the heat was really on him. If he were caught or detained or inspected with the designator in his possession, he would be arrested and interrogated. The odds of escaping from such a situation were minimal. He needed to get close to his area of interest and hide the case where only he would know where it was.

He decided on the way back to Esfahan that he would hide the case somewhere near the edge of the city. As he neared Esfahan, he traveled through a valley that was deserted, and about at the bottom of the valley, he stopped beside the road. He thought that anyone who saw him would think he was getting out to relieve himself, and he took the ditching tool and the box and his GPS with him as he strode into a clump of nearby bushes. Once concealed by the bushes, he quickly dug a hole and put the case in it. Then he covered it over and swept the sandy soil above it with a branch to obliterate the marks left by the ditching tool. Then he walked back to the Rover and got in. He took out his GPS and made a waypoint for his location. Close enough for him to quickly find the area where he had buried the case, but not so specific that someone who might capture him and the GPS could use the GPS to go back to the case. Only he knew exactly where the case was buried and that was that.

He started the motor and drove back into Esfahan to his rooming house. He parked the

Rover on a side street and walked the last quarter of a mile to the rooming house, but stopped at the market on the way to have some breakfast of boiled oats and dates and black coffee.

During the days, he would walk about Esfahan, learning what he could, but basically marking time until he was notified when and where to use the designator.

Chapter 41

The next day, Beri slept in until about nine, local time. He could not get to sleep the night before and finally got to sleep about one thirty. Instead of eating breakfast, he ate an apple that he had saved from the day before. Then he washed and dressed to go walk about a bit, all the time, waiting for instructions. He cell phone was encrypted and had a software lock. One had to input four digits correctly in order to be able to operate the phone or see anything it held. There was also a device built into it, that if a series of five numbers were input on the keypad, it would self-destruct in twenty seconds using a thermite charge. Once set, the phone should be put where it could not burn anyone.

He had left off some of his clothing at a laundry nearby and he walked there to retrieve it. Even though he could have carried on a conversation with the older lady who was working the counter, she simply looked up at him with a quizzical look and he handed her his ticket with the matching number on it. She retrieved the paper bag of folded clothes and told him the charge was Seventy five thousand rials, approximately three dollars. He gave her a one hundred thousand rial note and she gave him change. He nodded his appreciation and she smiled and he turned and walked into the scalding heat.

In his meanderings he came to a good sized market. There were several rows of merchants, selling everything from assorted beans and grains to small portable television sets. The smell of food being cooked wafted over the dusty crowd. Observing that the breeze was from the west, he turned into it and homed in on the food merchants' section of the market.

He picked a food merchant by the smell of its products and got in line to place his order. He was about fifth in line and people got in line after him. A man behind him spoke in a harsh voice, but obviously not meant for Beri.

"What are you doing here, unescorted? Don't you know the law?" he scolded. The lady behind Beri was very frightened by the two policemen who were glowering at her. He heard her say, "I am a scientist. I work for the Ministry of Science in the next block. There were no men to escort me and I need to eat and return to my station promptly," she said.

"You will have to come with us. We will check your story," one said.

On impulse, Beri turned and said in a sharp voice, "Leave her alone. She is with me."

Then he spoke to the woman, "If I had known you were coming here to eat, you could have come with me."

Then, turning to the officers, he said, "Leave her to me. I will see that she gets back to her station without being a problem to anyone."

Beri's steady gaze was enough to convince the policemen that they were dealing with someone who knew how to manage things and handle himself, so the shorter of them said, "Very well, sir, we will leave her in your custody, but admonish her not to come here again without escort or we will have no choice but to take her into custody."

"I will see that she is properly cautioned," said Beri. "Thank you for your courtesy."

The officers turned away and people parted to let them pass. Police there wielded a lot of authority and it was best not to cross them, so people avoided eye contact whenever possible.

After the police had gotten several yards away, she said, for the benefit of anyone standing close, "Thank you, Doctor Saleh, I did not know you were going to be here. I am very grateful."

"That is alright," said Beri. By this time, they were at the head of the line and the waiter looked at them to take their order. Beri ordered a hummus plate with pickles and green olives and naan bread and tea to drink. She ordered a lamb stew and a salad with vinegar and oil dressing and tea, likewise. The merchant had spread several small circular tables with folding metal chairs under a large tent covering, where they went and sat down.

By this time, they were both a bit nervous about the other. She spoke first. "My name is Mitra Borazjan. What I said to the officer is true. I am a scientist and I work at the Ministry building in the next block.

"My name is Beri Herzliya and I am a soldier on leave. I am an avionics technician and I usually work on jet aircraft." He noticed that she had green eyes when their eyes met while he was speaking.

After a few minutes of silence while they ate, she spoke again. "Thank you so much for coming to my aid back there. Those policemen can be so rude and officious sometimes. I think the rule that women cannot go about unescorted is so primitive. I became used to so many freedoms when I was in the United States in college. I hope women can achieve more rights here."

"I am a chemist," she said. "I went to college in the United States and returned here three years ago. I test water samples for the Ministry."

"That is a coincidence," he said. "I took my training at Embry Riddle University in Florida. The Republic paid for my tuition on the condition that I enlist for five years after college. It has been three years now."

"Are you stationed nearby?" she asked.

"Yes, I am on temporary duty at Hesa Air Base, but I had ten days of accumulated leave when I was transferred, so I thought I would look around a bit. I have five more days before I have to report."

By now, they both had become self-conscious that they had neither taken a bite of their meal. She ceased to look directly at him and focused on her plate of lunch.

"And yes," he said. "I enjoyed being in the United States, too, and I have had to be sent to other western nations for further training and to work on our aircraft. We have a large maintenance facility in Karachi. I really enjoyed the west. Tell me about yourself."

"I am thirty two, widowed, no children. I live with three other female employees of the Ministry in a house about a mile from here. My parents live in Qom and I was raised there. My father is a professor at the University there. My mother is a writer and an intellectual. They met at college and have been married for forty years. Tell me about yourself."

'You already know most of it. I am thirty four years old. I have been in the military all my adult life. My father was a bureaucrat in the government of the Shah. My mother was a cook in a local restaurant. I was raised in Beshehr. I got a scholarship to the military college and learned about aircraft and avionics there. I have an international certification as an avionics technician from the Federation Aeronautique in France, the international licensing agency. I was married, but my wife left me and we divorced seven years ago. I have no children."

"Is Beri your full name?" she asked.

"No, my full name is Huckleberry Finn," he said.

She guffawed and laughed, showing a mouth of perfect teeth. "What a beautiful woman," he thought. "Do you suppose she is actually following me and is not as innocent as she seems?" he asked himself.

"What a nice man," she thought. "Such a nice smile. I like him."

As they finished their lunch, they cast their paper plates and plastic cups into a nearby garbage can and walked back out into a shaded area. He said, "Just to fulfill my duties, let me escort you back to your work, then I will go."

She took his arm with a smile and they started the walk back to the Ministry.

Beri thought to himself as they neared the Ministry building. "Sometimes you get an accurate reading about someone by just walking a while with them. She seems so nice, but she is so beautiful, she must be thinking that I am not nearly good enough for her. On the other hand, she may have been sent to watch me or to entice me. I must be careful."

She was thinking, "What a nice man. I think he is handsome, and he has a gentle strength that I like. I wonder if he will be interested in me enough to ask to see me again?"

As they got to the stairs leading up to the first floor of the Ministry Building, she slipped her arm from under his and turned to face him. She said: "Thank you again, Beri, for the rescue. I am very grateful."

He said: "Don't you think it would be a more complete fulfillment of my duties as your escort if I would walk you home to your residence after work? I don't want to be thought of as less than diligent." He smiled. She smiled.

She said, "I finish my shift at four. I will meet you here."

He smiled and watched her go up the steps to the entry.

Chapter 42

Beri timed his walk to arrive at the Ministry building at four o'clock, so he would not be seen to be loitering around near the entrance. He walked up the street to the steps where he had left Mitra after lunch and slowed as he got within fifty yards. He glanced at his watch. It was four oh three and he continued to slowly walk up the street. As he got within twenty yards, she appeared at the door and came down the stairs. He sped up a bit to normal walking speed and met her just as she got to the bottom of the stairs.

"How nice of you to come for me," she said, politely for anyone nearby to hear.

She fell into step with him, just a little behind directly beside him, so observers could see that she was being properly respectful of her male escort. After they had gone a couple of blocks, she moved up and put her arm through his and pulled herself over closer to him.

"It is about a mile to my apartment. Could we stop and have a cup of tea or something on the way?" she asked.

He nodded and smiled.

As they walked, she said, "That tea house ahead is a good place."

They were shown to a booth set in the wall of the restaurant. The walls enclosed them on three sides. At last, they could enjoy a little privacy.

After they had been seated and relaxed a little, the waiter came to take their order. She ordered a pot of tea and a luncheon platter which, according to the menu which was handwritten on a stiff card, contained kabab lamb, hummus, steamed rice and stewed tomatoes, with naan bread and dates and figs.

While the waiter was fetching their meal, she put her hand on his and looked directly in his eyes and said, "Beri, I am attracted to so very few men. I can tell that I am drawn to you, but I think it best if we get some things straight right at the beginning. I want you to tell me what your goals are, what you political views are, what you like and don't like. If I am being forward, forgive me. I am not a loose-moraled woman. I just want to prevent myself from getting too attached to a man whose life will lead me away from my core beliefs and goals. I need to be comfortable with you to let you get closer to me. Do you understand?"

Beri was a bit startled by her frankness and her directness, but given the present political situation in Iran and all the turmoil in peoples' lives, he could understand. He became intensely aware of how soft her hand was, holding his. He felt his heart gallop a bit and he started to answer her.

"I was raised in a loving family. I have a younger sister who is married to an engineer and they have two boys. I am a little on the shy side, not what you would call a forward man, but I noticed something nice the first time our eyes met. I have no one in my life, no girlfriend or anything like that. Because of my job I have learned to be alone most of the time and I don't think I am very good at personal relationships. I feel clumsy, especially under these circumstances, because I want you to like me and I am a bit apprehensive that something I say or do will drive you away. You are very beautiful and might have dozens of suitors clamoring for your attention and I might be someone you will quickly discard when you get to know me a little better."

She smiled to indicate amusement and flattery and looked away for a moment.

At that moment, the waiter arrived with their tea pot and platter. The arrival broke their concentration for the moment and they tended to the filling of cups, adding lemon and honey and trying the platter's contents.

Beri was grateful that the lunch was so tempting because he sensed that he was stumbling and bumbling in the exchange. He felt clumsy and that he had overplayed his hand by saying what he had just said.

"Don't let down your guard," his conscience told him. "Be tough just now. She is so beautiful, but she could be an enemy, just sent to scout you out."

She gave him a soft look and said, "And what is to keep me from thinking that you are a womanizing cad who will tell a girl what she wants to hear and who cares not whom he hurts?"

"These are things we must find out about each other. Just telling you that I am not like that will be of no use."

She nodded feigning serious consideration, then gave him a beaming smile.

"You asked me how I felt about the present situation. Since I am in the military, my feelings might surprise you. I would leave this country and go to the west if I could. I despise being dictated to. I can see that our country is oscillating between a despotic shah and Muslim clerics who are every bit as brutal and dictatorial. The differences are not in how much they oppress our people, but in how the mullahs have alienated the rest of the civilized world. This is very hard on our people. Our people are so demoralized. Our young people cannot find work. There is no growth in the industrial sector. I sense that the outside world continues to pass us by. Even now, we have such a gap to make up. Such people are easy to manipulate and the mullahs take advantage of this to misdirect the anger and unrest of our people against distant foes, like Israel and the United States, when the faults of our country are right here in our government. If we had anything like the freedoms of the west, our people could thrive and be happy. I am very pessimistic about the future here. I feel helpless to do anything about it and I sense that most people feel the same."

She sat pensively for a bit, enjoying the tea and the platter of food.

After a pause, she leaned forward and asked him, almost is a whisper, "If you could leave and go to the west, would you?"

He took her hand and stared into her eyes. Then he said: "I have two more years in the army. I had not thought of actually leaving before that, but if I had someone to share my life with in the west, someone who believed as I do, someone I would be empty without, yes, I would go."

He paused for a long moment. Then said, "But, we are just dreaming. You have just met me. We don't know each other very well. Isn't this a bit nutty?"

"I have no idea," she said, with a sly smile. "But it is a sad comment on the present state of affairs that we must speak of politics before our first kiss."

"I know," he said. "It took a long time to get to this kind of state of affairs."

She said, "Besides, how do you know I don't have thick ankles?" smirking at him.

"Maybe you had better show me soon," he said.

"I hate these chadors. I loved being in the west where I could wear skirts and look like a woman. I loved the way westerners treated their women, too. No police harassment about being out alone without a male family member."

He looked at her with a serious expression. "Would you like to go back to the west, Mitra?

"Someday, in my dreams, I would like to go back, but they would never let me out now. Scientists are in such short supply, it would be impossible for me to get a VISA. They know that I do not have any relatives in the west and I have all the education they need me to have."

She seemed to have lost her appetite. He took another bite of his lunch while she just looked at him with a faraway look in her eyes. He wanted to tell her that he was not what he seemed, not what he had told her he was. He wanted to scoop her up, get on a white horse and gallop off into the sunset, toward the west, of course.

"If I ever get to go to the west again, I think I will settle in the southwest. The climate is hot, but dry and the scenery is magnificent. I found that I liked Mexican food, too."

They finished their meal and walked back to her house. At the gate to the perimeter wall, she took her hand from under his arm and turned to face him.

"It is best that we not have our first kiss here in the open. Perhaps tomorrow, if you will meet me after work, we could go to a nice restaurant for dinner and I will show you my ankles, if you promise not to laugh."

"I promise," he said. "See you at four tomorrow."

When he turned the turn at the corner, he looked back and she was watching him. He nodded and she nodded. He walked the two miles to his rooming house with a new purpose.

Chapter 43

After he had walked about a mile, he felt a
vibration in his pocket. He had set his cell
phone to vibrate, but instead of retrieving it
from his pocket, he simply kept walking, but
now at a faster pace.

When he got back into his room, he took off
his kefeyah and robe and sat heavily in the
only chair in the room, a big old leather
overstuffed red wing back, obviously from a
nice office or residence somewhere, but worn
almost completely out. The message on the
phone was a digital string. He copied down
the digits and then went to the codebook
feature in the phone. The phone had been set
up by General Haim's cryptography bureau
and had a vocabulary of terms and phrases
built into its vocabulary. If anyone tried to get
into it, though, the phone would erase itself
and become inert.

He put in his coded identifier and accessed
the vocabulary. There were over a hundred
terms and words, each corresponding to a
two digit or two character or combination of

digit and character code. He laid down the sheet with the numbers on it and wrote down what each combination translated to. When he finished, the message said: "Celebration on Friday." "Bushehr." "Eggs expected to hatch in late morning." "Provincial Capital." "Advise any time if you become unable to perform."

The message gave him three days to get to Bushehr and find a place to hide within view of the Provincial Capital. Tonight, he would go and dig up the duffel bag with all of his gear in it. Tomorrow, sometime, he would catch a bus for Bushehr. He had buried all of the sensitive equipment and his weapons in the duffel, carefully wrapped in a plastic garbage bag, behind a wall about a half mile from the rooming house. Since he had paid in advance for two weeks, he would simply leave the room locked and the television on, so the room would probably not be visited for several days. Transient workers like him would often leave such quarters in a like manner in this part of the world.

He got out his map of southern Iran and spread it on the small table in the room. He could see that the trip to Bushehr was about three hundred kilometers and would probably take the better part of a day, with all the stops the bus would make.

He decided to take a nap and get up later and buy dinner out, then go to retrieve the duffel. He also decided to be at Mitra's building at seven A.M. to try to see her to explain why he would not be meeting her that afternoon and to reassure her that he was not just skipping out.

When he awoke later, it was dark. His watch showed eight PM. He visited the bathroom at the end of the hall, and came back to assess things and get ready to leave. He was traveling light, with only a small satchel of necessities. The bulk of his stuff was in the duffel.

He made one more check of the room, even looking under the bed, and, satisfied that he was all together, he turned on the TV, with the volume low, locked the door as he left and slid the key under the door.

The small ditching tool in his satchel made the job a little longer to dig up the duffel than if he had had his regular ditching tool, which was in the duffel. When he retrieved the duffel, he wadded up the garbage bag and reburied it and smoothed the soil with a tree branch. At this point, it was a little after four A.M., so he walked slowly in the general direction of Mitra's building. It was early enough, so he decided to wait for her near her apartment and changed course.

At dawn, he was waiting about a hundred yards from her apartment, sitting on a low wall, next to the road. He waited patiently, and at about ten minutes to seven, she came out and walked toward him. When he saw her, he stood so she would recognize him.

As she walked up, she said: "What a pleasant surprise. I did not expect to see you until four P.M."

All he could think of to say was "Good Morning."

They fell into step along the road on the way to the Ministry.

After they had walked a little, she said, "I get the feeling that your baggage means that you are on your way. Will you be gone long?"

"My orders are to report right away for transport to Bandar Abbas. I would guess that it will be a temporary assignment of a few days, then back to Hesa Air Base."

"I see," she said. They walked silently for a few minutes.

Teasingly, she said, "At least if you are dumping me, you had the manners to come and give me some kind of explanation."

Even though he realized that she was kidding, he said: "Mitra, that is not my purpose at all. I want very much to get to know you better. I will be back in a few days. I will not be able to communicate with you, so when I get back, I will come to your apartment or the Ministry building, as you direct, and wait for you."

"If you are going to be that far away and in the presence of those lusty Bushehr women, I think you should at least find out if I have thick ankles," she said, taking his sleeve and pulling him toward an opening in a high wall along the road. The gap in the wall was wide enough for a large vehicle to pass through, but there was no gate. On the other side of the wall was a grove of lemon trees and the nearest tree afforded some shade and privacy. She had him stand about six feet away and coyly drew up her chador to show him her legs up to her knees. She posed a bit and turned her feet and ankles so he could see her ankles clearly in the morning light."

He did not know what to say or do, so he just smiled at her, and said: "Thank you."

She came over to him and took hold of his jacket front and pulled herself up close to him. She looked into his eyes and smiled, then drew him to her and kissed him very sweetly. He enjoyed it as much as she did.

Then, she gave his arm a pat and said, "Are my ankles too thick for you, Beri?"

Feigning studiousness, he said, "Well, I am not too sure. I need to inspect them more closely to be sure."

She laughed and swatted his arm.

As they went back to the opening in the wall, there was a step up to a level area just at the opening. He was beside her and she pulled up her chador a bit so she would not catch it on her shoe as she took the step up. Just then a large bus came by rapidly and the gust of wind caused by its passing blew her chador over her head. Beri got a chance to inspect a lot more than her ankles, then the gust died down and her chador settled once more over her.

She uttered a non-verbal indication of embarrassment and surprise and smoothed her chador once more.

"Well," she said. "That is a much more thorough presentation than I had planned. I hope you do not think less of me for revealing so much to you."

He said jokingly, "Oh, great, I meet a woman I really like and she turns out to be a flasher."

Now they both were laughing. Then he hugged her and said: "It was an accident, Mitra. You are quite beautiful. An unintended event has left me with an indelible and pleasant memory." He took her hand and led her back out the opening and down the road.

After a couple of minutes, she asked, "Have you always been an avionics technician? I got the impression from something you said that it was not your original duty."

"You are right," he said. "I was an attack helicopter pilot in the war with Iraq. Shortly before the truce, I was wounded by ground fire. I limped the helo back to base, but I had a head wound and after I recovered, the doctors discovered that I had balance problems, so I was relieved of that duty and retrained as an avionics technician."

"Do you still have balance problems," she asked.

"Only when a beautiful woman's chador blows over her head," he said.

She laughed and squeezed his hand and drew up next to him. As they walked he could feel her hip against his thigh every few steps. He liked the way she laughed. In fact, he had not found anything about her he did not like.

They arrived at the Ministry Building. Because of her position and the fact that she was a single woman, she could not show him any affection when they said their goodbye, so she simply extended her hands and he took them in his hands for a moment.

"Come back to me, Beri," she said.

"I will, Mitra. Take care."

She turned to go in and he turned to leave. It was a slow walk for them both.

Chapter 44

The message on her phone was waiting for her when Barbara awoke. It had come in the middle of the night and the vibrating phone did not wake her. Since her brother had already gone to work for the day, she had a time to work alone before his family would notice she was awake. She wrote down the two digit numbers and then accessed the code message feature. Once she had written down all the phrases, it read: "Expect the arrival south of your position. Others will act. Stand by. Expect to return according to the original plans."

"General, I think you had better come down here," the voice of Major Dev spoke from the phone. General Haim hung up and crossed the room to the door to his outer office.
"I will be gone for the rest of the day, Hermione," he said. "Reach me on the cell phone if anything comes up."

"Yes sir," the IDF female soldier replied. General Haim took his Buick and was at the cryptography bureau in a few minutes.

As he came in the door, Dev, who had been bent over a television screen, turned and motioned him over.

"Today is the day, General. Our people in place say that our fellow is going to be in Bushehr around noon and spend a couple of hours with local leaders. We think it is the opportunity we have been waiting for. I thought you would like to be here to see what is happening from our perspective."

"Yes, I would, Dev. Thanks. As far as I can tell, all elements of the plan are functioning properly. Our agent in Tehran has been told that she will not be part of the strike and to strand by. Our man in Esfahan has made his way by bus to Bushehr and has found a good place to hide. If the big cheese follows his itinerary, we may just have a chance to succeed here."

"We estimate the flying time at just a little more than an hour and a half, using the waypoints you gave us along the Saudi border and then across the Gulf."

"I believe we will have a better chance if we wait until we at least determine that he is enroute to the Provincial Capital. I think it would be better to plan the strike as he leaves, so we can hit the building if he is in there conferring with regional government officials or on the road if he leaves before our plane gets there."

"We have adjusted all coordinated clocks and everything is ready for the takeoff, General. Do you want to give the 'Go signal'?"

"Have we heard from out agent on the road to Beshehr?"

"No, sir, the best time information we have is the itinerary. He should be approaching Bushehr in an hour if he is on time."

"Is the bogus flight plan on file with air traffic control?" Haim asked.

"Yes, sir. The flight is booked as a training flight out over the Red Sea and return. No one but the men and women in this room and the officer at the revetment will know that the plane has no pilot on board. One of our men here will converse with clearance delivery, ground control, tower and departure control as if he were in the cockpit. Taxi and take off, as well as flight control will be done from this room, using the drone control console over there," he said, pointing to the console.

241

"Let's get this thing going, Dev. If we need the plane to loiter, we can do that over the desert and alter its arrival time by as much as forty minutes. I would feel a lot better to get that plane out of here."

"Very well, sir," said Dev and gave a thumbs up signal to an officer seated at the console in the rear of the room.

The officer, who was wearing a headset like he would be wearing if piloting a plane or working at air traffic control, reached up to his console and flipped a switch. A small green LED came on. He pressed a button switch on the control stick in front of him.

"Ovda Clearance delivery, Military four three six one five, in the north five revetment, is reporting in, ready for engine start in five minutes, requesting clearance according to flight plan."

"Roger, four three six one five. Stand by." There was a pause of about five seconds, then "Four three six one five, your flight plan is approved as filed. Expect twenty thousand ten minutes after departure. Fly runway heading on departure. Contact ground now on point niner."

General Haim asked Major Dev: "When will you switch control over from direct to the satellite link?"

Dev replied: "We are on the satellite link now, sir."

Haim, a bit surprised, but pleased, nodded.

The officer switched the communication radio to the ground control frequency, but hesitated. He dialed his cell phone. The answering officer was in the revetment at the north end of the field. "Go Charlie, engine start," said the officer. He knew the plan was to start the engine in the revetment and have it taxi out, then close the revetment front and back doors once the Mirage had cleared the revetment.

The silence of the revetment was punctuated by the whine of the starter motor in the jet's engine. It took several seconds to get the turbine up to the speed necessary to ignite fuel and begin to spool up to operating revolutions. A half a minute passed. The wheels were chocked and the Mirage was tied down as an additional precaution, in case the telemetry, which had been checked and rechecked, was off a bit and there was too much power being generated to safely taxi or the brakes did not hold.

The officer at the console, said into his cell phone. "Jeff, we can see on our instruments that you have engine start and all gauges are in the green. Pull the chocks and untie the ropes. We will hold the aircraft with its brakes as a test. Advise if the aircraft moves after you pull the chocks and untie the ropes."

Jeff made a hand signal to his two helpers to pull the chocks and untie the ropes. Once they did, the aircraft did not move.

"Ben, it looks good, the engine sounds good and the brakes are holding."

"Good, let's not waste any more fuel. Stand by for release."

"Okay," said Jeff and he pulled the start cart free of its connection with the Mirage. Now the pointy aluminum colored fighter was poised to go.

In a few seconds, the brakes released and the plane rolled forward out of the revetment. It turned left onto the taxiway and taxied east toward the active runway. Jeff and his two helpers rolled the front and back doors of the revetment closed and prepared to leave. As the Mirage taxied out of their sight, they locked the exit door and got into their Jeep Cherokee for the ride back to their office.

The officer controlling the Mirage could see what a pilot could see from the plane on a television receiver on his console. He stopped the Mirage with a lever that controlled its brakes at the edge of the second taxiway and called ground control.

"Ground, four three six one five is at the edge of Taxiway Echo, ready to taxi to the active Runway, with information Oscar."

General Haim smiled nervously. It was all coming together.

"Roger, four three six one five, taxi to Runway one six."

"Roger, four three six one five will taxi to Runway one six." said the controlling officer.

As he deftly taxied the Mirage to the runway threshold, Captain Nathan watched carefully in the viewer screen. It all looked good. He applied the brakes at the edge of the threshold of Runway one six as he stopped the Mirage perpendicular to the runway.

He switched the communications radio to tower frequency and called: "Tower, four three six one five is ready to go on runway one six."

"Roger, four three six on five, cleared to take off, maintain runway heading, squawk two three four five after departure and call approach on one two eight decimal five after departure. Have a good flight."

"Thanks, tower, six one five is rolling," responded Nathan and advanced the throttle to taxi onto the active runway and center the Mirage over the center stripe. Once on the center, Nathan advanced the throttle and the Mirage surged ahead. Six thousand feet down the runway, its nose wheel lifted and then the Mirage was airborne.

"Positive rate of climb, gear coming up," said Nathan so anyone nearby could hear.

"Approach, six one five, off runway one six, climbing through two thousand, squawking two three four five," Nathan said.

"Roger, six one five, radar contact, maintain heading of one six zero and climb to flight level two zero zero, advise reaching."

"Six one five, heading one six zero and up to flight level two zero zero and will advise."

Haim and Dev and Yakob exchanged cautious smiles and nods.

Chapter 45

Beri had ridden the night bus from Esfahan to Bushehr. It lumbered through the night, stopping several times. Only a disciplined sleeper could have gotten a good night's sleep that night. But, about seven AM, the bus pulled into the station in east Bushehr. Beri got his duffel and slung it on his shoulder and walked west toward town. As soon as he was out of sight of the bus station and felt that he was not being followed, he turned south on the first major street he came to. There was a minor market in the square about a block away and there were a few taxicabs waiting for fares. He had consulted his map of Bushehr on the bus and decided to ask the driver to take him to an address just north of the Provincial Capital. Since he knew that virtually no one outside of the military would know that the Grand Ayatollah would be paying a visit to the Provincial governor today, he felt secure in using an address a couple of blocks north and west of the Capital. He paid the driver and picked up his duffel again and started walking westerly. Once the taxicab was out of sight, he went over to a low wall and sat down, both to rest and to get a feel for the area and maybe pick a good spot to hide.

It became obvious that the buildings on the west side of the main road were taller than those on the east side, so he decided to go over to the west side of the main highway to see if he could find a place to hide. As he walked, he gave thought to how he might get out of the area afterwards. What was about to occur was a major event and the area would soon be crawling with police and military.

He walked back to the market and bought a melon and a gyro type sandwich of mutton and a sauce made with sour cream, olive oil and wine vinegar and spices. It was delicious and he enjoyed a bottle of water afterward and a couple of figs. He sat on a shipping crate to eat, since no one seemed to mind. Then, he picked up his duffel and a bag of his lunch garbage and threw the garbage into a burning barrel of trash as he passed on his way east.

He walked the two blocks to the main highway and, after carefully observing to the north and south, as if being cautious about crossing, he crossed. He had noticed that he was about a half kilometer from the Provincial Capital, but he did not stare.

Once safely on the other side of the road, he began to walk north and south on the next street over parallel with the highway, looking for a place to hide. One thing he really wanted to find was a building two or three stories tall that had a clear view of the Provincial Capital and the highway. Resting every twenty minutes or so, he walked for more than two hours on his search.

Once when he was resting, he began thinking about Mitra. She was intelligent, pretty, educated, politically suitable and had a wonderful sense of humor. He knew he would want to continue to see her. He laughed to himself when he thought about the chador blowing over her head. How very beautiful she was in that fleeting moment. It might have been a long time before he saw that much of her in a normal courtship, but they laughed it off and went on.

As he mused, he looked up and, across the street, facing east, was an old building. It had a one car garage door on the ground floor and what looked like a small apartment above.

He sat and watched it for several minutes. Then, he decided to have a closer look. He got up and slung his duffel onto his shoulder and ambled across the road and walked past the building. It sat with its front about twenty feet back from the edge of the road. The windows in the upstairs were dirty and one was broken, but not displaced or missing glass. He went down the road into the next block and crossed the street again. On the far side, he found a low wall and sat down with his duffel beside him. He watched the building for half an hour or more. The adjacent buildings appeared to house small shops, one obviously a butcher shop and the other appeared to be a bakery. He noticed that all three of the buildings backed up to an alley that was only wide enough for a person to walk through, not nearly wide enough for a car.

After he had watched long enough, he got into his duffel and made sure that a coil of rope was just inside the zipper opening. Then he hoisted it again and crossed the street and walked slowly toward the building. The neighborhood was quiet, with only a few people on the street. No one seemed to be paying any attention to him. He turned beside the bakery and went back to the rear of the building. Then he turned into the alley and walked past the middle building. There was a window in the back of the second floor in addition to the two windows on each side. The front only had one window, too. He made a mental note of thanks that what he was about to do would not cause any loud noises that might attract attention to his hiding place. He walked the entire length of the alley, but did not go out the far end. He stopped short and then peeked out each way to see if anyone were looking in his direction. He stayed a minute or two and tried to be thorough to see if anyone could look up the alley. When he felt secure, he went back to the building in the middle. He put his duffel down and unzipped it and took out the rope. He tied one end around the handles of the duffel and the other end around his waist. Then he put his feet on the opposite wall and, using his hands and feet alternately, walked himself up the wall. When he got up as far as the window, he stopped when his eyes were only high enough to peer into the lowest edge of the window. The inside appeared to be a store room. There were large and small cardboard boxes and stacks of clothing and old furniture. He was relieved to find that it was not someone's residence. The window was latched, but he took his knife from his pocket and used it to reach up between the sashes and move the lock. He gripped the knife in his teeth and pushed the lower sash up enough to crawl through. Then, he eased over and reached over the ledge at the bottom of the window and pulled himself up over and into the building. He quickly leaned back out and reeled in the duffel. Once he got it up and inside with him, he quietly lowered the window. By now, he was soaking wet with exertion and apprehension. He took a while to wind down.

Once he felt a little more relaxed, he started to explore the room. It had a bare, unfinished wood floor and the inside walls were of the same material as the outside of the walls. He looked again at his watch. Ten twenty five. There was no ceiling of the room. The joists for the ceiling were open and he could see all the way to the interior surface of the roof.

For security reasons, he knew not to use his cell phone, so he took out of his satellite phone the lead lined tube he was to use to aim it upward. That way, no transmissions would leak out and the beam of the phone would be directed upward only. There was no way for him to tell if there were a satellite that could receive his transmission, but he decided to try anyway. If he were not successful, he could try again in half an hour, or every ten minutes, for that matter.

Using the code feature in his modified cell phone, which could be used without activating its reception and broadcast mode, he composed a message. Then he wrote down beside each message the two digit code for that message. The message, decoded, was: "In place. Bushehr. Half click N of PC. Awaiting instructions."

He held his breath and turned the satellite phone on. He quickly aimed it upward and transmitted the pre-recorded digital message and just as quickly turned it off. He looked at his watch and noted the time. In ten minutes, he could expect a reply if they received his message. He used the ten minutes to build himself two little nests in the front of the room, one to be used at the front-most side window and one out the only front window.

In ten minutes, he turned on his cell phone again. In about thirty seconds, came a series of two digit numbers and characters. He copied them down and used the decoding feature to partially decode the message. He wrote the coded message on a scrap of cardboard he found. The message read: "Santa Claus is coming to town. Oh, what a beautiful morning. Twin reindeer. White horses. Will Kane would know." This message meant that the Grand Ayatollah was indeed coming to Bushehr. In the morning, this morning. He would be in a two car convoy, (very low profile), and would be in white vehicles. Strike estimated at noon. (The reference to Will Kane was from the movie "High Noon.")

Beri looked at his watch. It was ten forty five. He had work to do.

Chapter 46

He inspected the room he had broken into. It was about twelve feet wide and about thirty five feet long. It comprised the entire second floor of the building. He noticed that there was no door to an outside stairway. How would he get out,? He wondered. On the north side of the room, about half way back from the front windows, there was a trap door in the floor. It was about three feet wide and five feet long, along the north wall. It was smooth with the existing floor, but had a hole about an inch and a half in diameter in the middle of its south side. He put his index finger in the hole and pulled. The door revealed a ladder which led down to the main floor. There were no windows on the first floor, so he showed his flashlight down into the room below. It was dusty and there were several large items covered with sheets of canvas looking fabric. One large item had the look of a vehicle, so he went down the ladder and looked around. Sure enough, when the pulled up the cover, there was a vehicle. It was an old beat up Mazda pick-up truck. The bed of the truck was full of boxes of household items, like dishes and glasses and small rugs rolled up and an old split bottom chair.

"It would be a nice getaway vehicle," he thought. "I wonder if it will start." He spent some time removing the canvas cover and cleared some space in front of the truck so he could check it over. Without a key, the only way he could check to see if there were gasoline in the tank would be to probe the tank filler with some kind of item to see if there was fuel or to hot wire the ignition to see what the gauge read. He chose to hot wire the ignition. He pulled the wires from the ignition switch and showed the flashlight on them. Four wires, black, white, red and blue. He touched the black and white wires together. There was a small spark and the gauges swung. The fuel gauge indicated about half full. He pushed the gear shift lever into neutral, pulled on the hand brake to be sure it was set and touched the red wire to the black and white wires. The starter turned, but slowly. He arranged the wires so they could not touch each other and got out to check further. He quietly raised the hood of the truck and checked the battery terminals. They were pretty corroded, but were tight enough. He checked the fluid in the cells of the battery and they were Okay, too. He pulled the engine dip stick and found the oil level was normal and the oil was dark enough that it indicated it was nearing time when it would need to be changed . All in all, it was good enough to use and would make a good getaway vehicle.

Since the "main event" was about to occur, he decided to go ahead and try to start the truck. If the battery were down, he could let it run a bit to charge up the battery. If it would not start, it was best he know it now.

On the first try, the started cranked over the engine slowly at first, but gained some speed after the oil began to be circulated. After about ten seconds, he quit and waited a minute. On the second attempt, the engine started and settled into a lumpy idle. He gave it a bit of throttle and it smoothed out at about twelve hundred revolutions per minute. He ran the engine for about five minutes, to warm the oil, get it circulating and to charge the battery a bit. He noticed that the voltmeter indicated a healthy charge. He shut it down and got out.

He decided to clear the path in front of the truck so he could take it. In front of the truck, sitting with its long axis across the path of the truck, was a canvas covered article about four feet tall. He pulled off the canvas cover and discovered an old motor scooter. It was a Vespa and looked like it had had a full life.

The paint was worn off on the foot rests on each side. The handles were well worn, but it was all there and looked serviceable. He pulled the cover clear of the Vespa and gave it a closer check. The oil in the crankcase was rather clean, considering. He pumped the starter pedal slowly several times to circulate oil and to see if he detected any roughness indicating the bearings were shot. It turned freely, so he pumped it about a dozen times, slowly. Then he switched on the ignition switch and gave the starter pedal a hearty kick. The little scooter gave a chuff of smoke and a muffled pop. He kicked it again. Same result. He kicked it a third time and the engine fired. It ran roughly for about ten seconds and then settled down. A cloud of blue smoke came from its exhaust pipe. He let it run for about a minute, during which it settled down to a nice idle. Then, he shut off the switch and rolled the scooter aside to clear the path for the truck. Now he had the option to take either one. He looked at his watch. Ten fifty five. He walked over to the door and made sure that he could unlatch and raise it when he wanted to, but he did not move it. Then, he went back up the ladder to his hide out.

He decided to watch out the front window for the time, and got into the nest he had created there. He got out a couple of energy bars from his satchel and a bottle of water. As he munched the first bar, he noticed a pair of white Toyota Land Cruisers approach from the north. They did not seem to be in a hurry and just kept up with the lazy traffic in the road. He was a block away from the road on which they would pass, so he got out his binoculars to have a better look. The first vehicle had what appeared to be four people aboard. Nothing unusual. No weapons apparent. The second vehicle hung back just enough that the casual observer would not conclude that the two vehicles were traveling in a convoy. It looked normal, too, except that the rear windows were tinted. There were two men in the front seat, but he could not see more than that.

He got up and went to the south side window and followed the vehicles down the road. The buildings along the road obscured the vehicle from time to time, but he could see them as they approached the Provincial Capital, then they passed in front of a building that blocked his view. He looked at his watch. Eleven eleven.

He took out his cell phone and looked up a couple of code phrases. He then hurriedly broadcast them. When Major Dev and General Haim received the message, they tensed. It said, in code, "Hen is on the nest. Advise."

Beri kept his binoculars on what he could see of the Provincial Capital. A few minutes passed. The phone buzzed. He noticed that the vibration made a tiny cloud of dust on the burlap sack where he had laid it. He picked it up and looked at the code message. He wrote down the digits and symbols. The message said: "Underway. ETA sixty five minutes. Advise if necessary to adjust ETA later."

Beri quickly composed and sent a response. "Proceed. Will advise."

General Haim and Major Dev looked at each other without expressing their thoughts. Both knew what was about to occur.

Chapter 47

The phone made it easy to conceal the information. The coded message meant: Santa Claus (the Grand Ayatollah) is coming to town. Rudolph is fifteen today meant that the team expected the Mirage to arrive in fifteen minutes. Big mac meant two story building (Double decker). Top hat meant building with flag pole on top. One half click meant half a kilometer.

Lero quickly got out the laser designator. He sent Jean with Zabol to wait about a kilometer away to the north, the opposite direction from the two story building with the flag pole on top. They had previously scouted out a place to meet in case they got separated. It was a large market and there was an adjacent vacant field where people parked cars and left wagons with mules and horses. There were always people coming and going and it was a good cover. Only late at night would it be vacant.

He had but a moment to give Jean a hug and see them out of the suite.

Lero knew that the large building down the road was the office of the Provincial Governor. The flag on top reminded him of the directions he had received. He took out the case with the Collins Flight Director in it and put it on the table. With his miniature electric screwdriver, he took the right panel off of the flight director case.

He went around the table to be able to see out the open window in the direction of the building south of him. There was only one building that met the description of two story with a flag pole on top. He returned to the case and removed the components of the laser designator from their hiding places inside the case of the Collins Flight Director. and put them on the table. Next, he opened the case with the Garmin GPS navigation system in it and removed the battery for the designator. In a minute he had assembled the designator and set up his tripod with the telescope to spot his target.

He was glad that Jean was far enough away to not be at risk. He noticed that his palms were beginning to sweat and his mouth was dry.

As he looked through the telescope which was pointed at the building down the road, he noticed that people had begun to congregate out front. Probably the word had gotten out that the Grand Ayatollah was paying a visit to the Governor and people wanted a glimpse of their leader.

Since the Israeli agent was to designate the target and Lero was only to stand by in case it did not work out, he put on his specially tinted glasses to pick up the spray of light from the Israeli agent's designator, which would tell him that he need not use his designator. He got out the thermite charge, so he could destroy the designator if necessary and attached it to the case of the designator.

His cell phone vibrated again. He wrote down the digits again. When he checked them they said: "Definite. Second horse. Cinco de Mayo." This meant the strike was on. The second horse meant that the Grand Ayatollah would be riding in the second vehicle if he left the building. Cinco de Mayo meant that the Mirage was only five minutes out. Lero knew that in the thick air near sea level, the Mirage would be capable of about eleven hundred miles per hour, most probably faster than anything in the Iranian air force. The plan had been for the approach to be at full speed and in a shallow dive the last ten miles. Five minutes at eleven hundred miles per hour meant that the airplane was now about ninety miles out. He could imagine the drone operators sweating in their booth in the second sub-basement at Ovda. He could imagine that the Iranians might have detected a fast moving intrusion. They may have even alerted the Ayatollah's security men that there might be a threat and urged them to move him from the Provincial Capitol.

As Lero watched, the double doors of the building opened and a group of people came out. The locals pressed close until the police restrained them. A small group got into the first and second vehicles.

"Now the entourage was in the vehicles and they began up the street toward Lero's position. At first the crowd of onlookers prevented the vehicles from going very fast, but when the crowd thinned out a bit, they accelerated some. The vehicles were coming right toward Lero's position.

Lero did not know, of course, where the Israeli agent was, or even if he was in a position where he could paint the building or the vehicles. It was only two minutes now until the expected strike. The vehicles had departed the building and were coming toward him.

One minute now. Lero knew that the Israeli agent would be painting the target now if he were able. There was no light or spray coming from the vehicles, so Lero decided to energize his designator. He began painting the vehicles, and the second one, in particular, when it was in view. On they came. They were now about a quarter of a mile away. No other designator signal was visible.

"Any time now," he thought. Then it occurred to him that the vehicles might get to the front of the hotel just as the Mirage did, which would wipe out the building as well as the vehicles. There was no time to change the plan. He kept the designator aimed at the vehicles. Sweat was dripping down his forehead and occasionally getting in his eyes. Now the vehicles were three hundred yards away and picking up speed.

"Come on. Where are you?" he thought, wondering why the Israeli agent was not painting the target.

This was now what combat soldiers call "danger close," when they call in an airstrike or artillery barrage near enough to their position to put them is jeopardy. Usually the procedure is for the soldier and the pilot or artillery man to exchange names in case there needs to be discussion later or an investigation.

As he watched in acute fascination, a silver streak came into his field of vision from the right, behind the hotel. There was a tremendous fireball as the bombs and the plane hit the pavement next to the vehicles. In half a second the blast wave hit the hotel. The balconies were sheared off and fell to the street. The front wall was caved in on each floor and the whole front half of the hotel collapsed into a heap. Lero saw the bright day light become gray with flying debris and dust and then he was propelled back against the wall of his suite. As he hit the wall, the ceiling collapsed and everything went black.

Chapter 48

Where Jean waited with Zabol, everyone heard the blast. At a mile away, it took four seconds for the sound to reach them. They immediately looked over in the direction of the Provincial Capital and saw a tremendous fireball and smoke and debris flying up into the air. In another second the shock wave reached them, still strong even though a mile away. Everyone was transfixed. People then began looking around in fright, gathering their loved ones to make sure everyone was okay. Then they began to point and to express grief and fright at what they were seeing. Had it been another terrorist bombing, another opposition group trying to call attention to the plight of the people and disrupt the mullahs?

Zabot and Jean got in the taxicab and took a circuitous route around several blocks before they headed toward the hotel where they had left Lero. When they got near, they were unable to get within a block due to the chaos of people fleeing, people surging toward the site to find out what had happened and a few first responders trying to get to the scene, too.

When they rounded a corner and got a glimpse of the hotel, they stopped and gasped. The whole front of the five story hotel had collapsed. Smoke, fire and debris littered the street in front of what had been a nice looking building. The front half of the building had been demolished. To their left, down the road, there was complete chaos. There were people running in every direction. There was still a great cloud of smoke and ash. People were beginning to dig into the wreckage of the hotel, but when they moved large pieces of debris, more would come caving in. An ambulance passed in front of them on its way to the center of the disaster. It was surreal. The people who had been close had been deafened by the blast and they were shouting to each other because they could not hear. Many people were in shock. Many were coming toward them with bloody clothing and holding their heads and limbs.

As grim as it looked, neither Jean nor Zabol could make themselves believe that they had lost Lero. They hoped that somewhere in that pile of debris, the rescuers would find him alive. They decided, for security's sake, to back off and find a place to hide out until they could come back later and check on Lero.

The Red Crescent (the middle-eastern equivalent of the Red Cross) had set up an aid station on the west side of the road about a half mile north of the hotel. They found it was a good place to wait. They each took a large Styrofoam cup of tea from the aid workers and sat on a bench to wait a while. They saw an Al Jazeerah television van go by toward the site of the blast.

They waited for a couple of hours, then could wait no more. They got in Zabol's taxicab and drove toward the blast site.

General Haim and Major Dev watched in amazement as the Iranian coast swept into view on the screen. The nose camera showed Bushehr clearly. It was so fast that it was surreal As they watched, the sensors in the nose of the plane detected the laser designator and homed in on the beam splashing on the vehicles moving along the highway. As is hurtled closer, the plane seemed to focus on the second vehicle. In just a few moments, the plane crossed the seashore and dove even closer to the ground, coming in at about a five degree slope. Dev had set the throttle at max power. In the last few seconds, they could see the light

270

bouncing off of the Toyota Land Cruiser. In a moment, they could see the vehicle almost fill the screen, then the screen went into a snowstorm of black and white squares. Both men realized that they were sweating profusely. They looked at each other grimly. Dev was sitting and Haim was standing behind him, with his hands on Dev's shoulders. In a few seconds, discipline took over, each heaved a sigh of relief and apprehension.

"Dev, dismantle this console and scatter the equipment you have used on this strike. Go back to your regular routine and I will come to see you in a few days. I cannot thank you and the few men who worked on this enough. Ari would have been gratified. Take care of yourself. Tell your guys to keep their heads down. I will be in touch."

With that, he patted Dev on the shoulder and turned for the door. It wasn't until he got in the Buick that the gravity of what had happened hit him. He sobbed with relief. As soon as he could wipe the tears from his eyes, he started the Buick and drove back up the perimeter road to his office.

Chapter 49

"Ladies and gentlemen, we have just received a news flash, courtesy of Al Jazeerah Television. Dateline Bushehr, Iran. A large explosion occurred in south Bushehr at one thirty seven PM Local time today. Several vehicles and buildings were destroyed and there were numerous casualties. Local authorities have not released the identities of the victims, but the explosion occurred about a kilometer north of the Provincial Capital building just south of the center of Bushehr. The mysterious explosion left a smoldering crater ten feet deep in the street and only shards of torn metal strewn about. There were no reports of the number killed, however numerous casualties flooded local hospitals as several adjacent buildings were collapsed by the blast. Authorities are combing the wreckage to determine if the explosion was the result of a road side bomb or whether a missile was the cause. Witnesses report hearing a whistling sound just before the explosion and one man said he saw a silvery object going toward the vehicles. We will have more information as it becomes available."

Chapter 50

As they got near the hotel, they were stopped by a police roadblock. Zabol told the officers that they were returning to the Askari Hotel when the blast occurred and their associate, a French national was believed to be at the hotel, waiting for them. The guard let them through and they drove about half a kilometer toward the hotel before the crowd of fire engines, ambulances and the crowds of people digging into the rubble of homes and businesses prevented them from driving any farther. They walked up to the hotel. The entire façade of the hotel was collapsed and the front half of the building had caved in. Workers were climbing over the rubble and throwing pieces aside in an attempt to find people. Zabol told the person who seemed to be in charge that he was trying to find a Frenchman who was staying at the hotel on the third floor. He gave a description to the foreman who then directed his workers, male and female, to look for Lero among the piles of bricks and broken pieces of plaster and wood. The city had provided a medium sized end loader which was lifting piles of bricks and plaster debris from the front of the hotel and putting it in a pile out by the road. It was slow going, but people were probing the wreckage and calling out to see if any survivors could hear them. People were crying frantically for their loved ones in the hotel. It was chaos. Zabot and Jean took gloves and joined the line of workers handing pieces of rubble out to the street. Once, Jean stood up on a section of a wall and looked south down the road. There was still a large crowd of people surrounding the place where the blast had taken place. A fire continued to burn near the site. There were pieces of debris, large and small, littering the road. People were pushing the large pieces aside to allow ambulances and fire trucks to get in and were throwing the smaller pieces to the side of the road.

Jean and Zabol worked until they were very tired. Then they asked the foreman if they could be excused and went back to the taxicab. They went to another nearby hotel to see if they could get a room, so they could use the bathroom and rest a bit. There was only one room with a single bed available, so they took it. Zabol insisted that Jean take the bed and get some rest. After she visited the bathroom at the end of the hall, Zabol went and then came back and laid down on the floor and they slept for several hours.

When Jean awakened, it was the middle of the night. She called to Zabol, who woke instantly and sat up. They decided to get something to eat and drink and return to the hotel to see how the rescue attempts were going.

By the time they got to the hotel, it was about four AM. They reported to the foreman, who was expecting them, but who was a substitute for the man earlier encountered. He told them that they had located Monsieur Roman, but that he was badly injured. Doctors had started an IV for him and they were bringing him out on a stretcher.

As the six men lifted the stretcher out of the rubble and used a rope to prevent it from getting away from them on the unstable debris, they got their first glimpse of him. He was unconscious and there was a bloody bandage on his head. The medic who helped bring him down, told them that they had found him under a part of a wall that had collapsed. His right leg was broken below the knee, both bones, and he was thought to have broken ribs and a punctured lung. His breathing was being aided by oxygen, but he needed hospital treatment.

Jean's cell phone vibrated in her pocket. She motioned to Zabol that they needed to back away for a moment. When they were clear of the crowd, she told him about the cell phone call and looked at the digits on the screen. She wrote them down and decoded them each. The message read: "Air ambulance to arrive at approx seven AM local. Transport to Dubai for medical treatment." When Jean saw what the decoded message said, she sobbed on Zabol's shoulder.

By now, they had Lero at the door to the waiting ambulance. Jean and Zabol went over and identified themselves to the driver and attendant and got into the ambulance with Lero. She told the driver that an air ambulance was coming for Lero at the airport, so the driver eased the ambulance out of the debris laden area in front of the hotel and turned north on the main road.

Chapter 51

In his best French, Jefe called the Iranian
Embassy in Athens. Pretending to be a
second vice consul in the French embassy in
Athens, he expressed his profound grief at
the damage and loss of life in Bushehr, but
asked if he could have a Red Cross aircraft
airlift an injured French national so he could
get medical treatment at a hospital in Dubai.
The officer he spoke to thanked him for his
sympathy and said he would pass on his
request to his charge d'affairs and he could
call back in an hour to get the answer. Jefe
thanked the man and hung up.

Next, he dialed the American Red Cross
office in Rome. Still pretending to be a French
diplomat, he asked if the Red Cross had an
air ambulance that could pick up a wounded
French national and his assistant in Bushehr.
He related that the man had been in a hotel
near the blast and that the hotel had
collapsed on him and others.

"Regrettably, no, we do not have any aircraft
available. Can you find a private charter?"

"I will have to try. Thank you very much anyway." He hung up.

He got out his satellite phone and dialed a number he knew by heart. The phone buzzed characteristically then began ringing. On the third ring, a voice answered.

"Good afternoon," the voice said.

Jefe said, "This is Jefe. I need to know if we have an aircraft at Incerlik capable of intercontinental flight. I need an aircraft that has civilian markings. If you have a white plane, all the better. Could you paint a red cross on both sides and fly it to Bushehr with pilots in civilian clothes, to pick up a man and woman to evacuate them for medical treatment?"

"I will have to check and call you back. Thank you."

"Thank you, too," said Jefe.

(In Farsi, but with a French accent) (Even though English is the international language of air traffic control, many countries, including Iran, welcome the native language.)

"Bushehr control, Red Cross Delta Mike Yankee Delta, fifty miles out, landing Bushehr, on a mercy mission."

"Red Cross Delta Mike Yankee Delta, landing clearance approved, squawk 2121 and ident for us please. Plan straight in to runway one two at Bushehr. Information Mike is current."

Ahead, the pilots could see the Iranian coast clearly. Lights strung out to each side of Bushehr for many miles. It looked like a diamond necklace strung out along the coast. At about twenty miles, they made out the beacon at the airport and radioed control that they had the field in sight. Daylight was just coming to the region.

"Red Cross Delta Mike Yankee Delta, contact Tower now on one one eight decimal seven. Good morning."

"Yankee Delta, over to tower, thank you. Good morning."

"Tower, Red Cross Delta Mike Yankee Delta with you, field in sight."

"Roger Yankee Delta, cleared to land runway one two. Useful length three thousand meters. Wind is seven knots from zero six zero, pressure is three zero zero one."

"Thank you, tower. Yankee Delta."

The Cessna Citation landed as planned on runway one two and taxied to the ramp. Ground control responded with instructions to taxi to the white building beside the main terminal. As they got close, they could see the ambulance waiting.

"Ground, Yankee Delta will need to top up fuel with Jet-A."

"Roger, Yankee Delta. Will advise the fixed base operator. Welcome to Bushehr, of the Islamic Republic of Iran."

The drive to the airport took forty minutes. At the gate, the driver told the guard about Lero and Jean and Zabol and they were let through. They drove to the smaller white building by the main terminal. When they came to the building, the driver had his attendant go in and tell the personnel there that they were waiting for an air ambulance to arrive for their patient. As Jean and Zabol watched, a fuel truck lumbered over toward them. Since it was a private flight, they were given no announcement like a commercial flight. In about half an hour, the white Citation came taxiing up and shut down in front of them. The attendant and pilots got out and came over to the ambulance. The driver confirmed that their patient was Mr. Roman, whom they came to retrieve. As the fuel truck ground crew refueled the plane, they carefully loaded Lero into the cabin. In ten minutes, they were ready to go. Jean only had a brief time to speak to Zabol and thank him.

"Thank you, Zabol. We owe you so much," she said.

"I am glad I could help, Jean. Take good care of Lero. Remember, you have a friend in Iran."

She hugged him briefly, then turned and walked quickly to the waiting plane. The ground crew was just finishing with the fueling when she got to the plane, so she boarded without hesitation. She could see his dark eyes looking at her with concern as they shut the door and the starboard engine began to spool up.

"Ground, Red Cross Yankee Delta is at the fixed base operator, ready to taxi for departure to Dubai, with the numbers."

"Roger, Yankee Delta, taxi to runway one two, use taxiway Foxtrot, squawk 4355 on departure, expect one zero, ten thousand ten minutes after departure, over to tower now on one one eight decimal seven."

In just a few minutes, Yankee Delta received take off clearance and sprinted down the runway.   Fifty miles out, it changed course to Doha, Qatar. Jean held Lero's hand the whole way back.

Chapter 52

Beri heard a swooshing screaming sound just before the explosion. The explosion was so close that the building he was in was blown apart. The roof came off and was flung to the next street. The sides collapsed away from the blast and he fell through the floor to the room below. The last thing he remembered was the terrible shearing, groaning sound of the building collapsing. Then everything went dark.

Since the building was unoccupied, as people thought, no one came to look for Beri. When he regained consciousness, about an hour after the blast, he was in the dark. What lay above him completely cut off the light. Since he did not know how long he had been unconscious, he did not know if it were night or day anyway. He found that he had landed next to the old truck on boxes of household stuff, shoes, clothing and boxes and bags of beans and flour. He could not move much, but he was not badly injured. He began by trying to get things off of him so he could move more. In a few minutes, he was able to pull a large section of wall board toward him and when he did so, he could see a shard of light peeking through. It seemed that each time he moved an object or piece of debris, several other pieces shifted as they followed the drive of gravity. It took him what he estimated was an hour to make a hole big enough to get out from under the debris. When he cleared himself of his debris prison, he could see that the building had simply folded backwards with the blast and the walls lay like some giant hand had simply pushed the building rearwards until it collapsed.

He reasoned that his duffel would be somewhere near where he fell, so he went back into the debris and looked for it. He found it by feel more than sight and, working it back and forth several times, freed it from the grasp of the broken boards and siding that lay on top of it. He pushed the duffel out the hole he had escaped through. When he got the duffel out, he checked it to make sure there were no incriminating things in it. The laser designator was nowhere in sight, so he simply pulled the duffel out of the wreckage and found a place to sit and rest. He got a bottle of water out of the duffel and doused his face with part and drank the rest. He ate a couple of energy bars and that made him feel a bit better. By now, he was feeling the bruises and sprains caused by the fall and the collapse of the debris onto him. He thought it would be better to stand so he could assess how badly he was banged up and to determine if he could walk a bit.

There was not much use in depending on his right arm for lifting, so he tried to swing the duffel onto his left shoulder. The pain when the duffel settled on his right shoulder was piercing and he gave an involuntary squeal of pain. He thought he would black out. He saw bright spots and dark spots, and he staggered as he stood there.

In spite of the pain, he knew that he needed to put distance between him and the blast area, so he slowly trudged to the west, away from the collapsed building and toward the next north-south road. He could see an aid station ahead in the next neighborhood, but he chose not to stop there. Distance was what he craved and he pushed himself to walk about a half kilometer before he had to put the duffel down and rest. He took a bottle of water from his duffel and swallowed two pain pills.

After resting a bit, he got back up and slung his duffel and trudged up the road. From the road, at times, he could see the Gulf to his left. As he made another kilometer, he noticed a bus stop sign and decided to wait for a bus.

The local bus, like many others in the area, smelled of unwashed bodies and goats. The riders in this area were mostly going into downtown Bushehr and had come from rural areas to the south.

As he rode, he thought of all the reasons why he should try to escape in the Bushehr area and not go back to Esfahan. It was on the shore of the Gulf. Waterborne pickup would be relatively straight forward. Much more complicated to find his way to the border or the Gulf from Esfahan. Besides, she might turn him down. She might have better sense than he. She might opt to stay where she was, relatively safe, and seek an exit later, perhaps with a VISA to visit the U.S.. She might not feel the potential in their relationship that he felt. Besides, it was early in their relationship. It might go nowhere. She might not be what he thought. There was the remote possibility that she was a government agent, whom he had met by chance, but who would turn him in if he revealed his true identity to her. All these things muddled in his mind as the rode toward the middle of Bushehr.

He stayed on the bus until it reached the main bus terminal. He bought a plate of dinner at the restaurant next door and waited for the bus. The hot mutton stew tasted good and he bought a couple of bottles of water, one to drink then and one to carry on the bus. Even though he was well fed, he bought a sack of naan when he paid for his dinner and tucked it into his duffel.

After dinner, he went back over to the bus terminal. It was the moment of truth, so to speak. Now was his chance. He could hide out here in Bushehr, notify his people that he wanted picked up along the shore, or perhaps get out some other way. Or, he could take the risk of returning to Esfahan and telling Mitra enough to let her make an educated decision about leaving with him. He thought about whether to tell her he was really in Israeli. It would be a very decisive moment. Still, the prospect of her was tempting. She was so very much like what he needed. "Besides," he thought, with a laugh, "She does not have thick ankles." Far from it. He remembered what she looked like with her chador coyly withdrawn to her knees and what she looked like in that fleeting moment when the bus blew her chador over her head in the lemon grove. That memory would live with him permanently, he knew.

"So here we are," he thought. The ticket booth was fifty feet from the bench where he had sat down with his duffel. The place was dusty and smelled of sweat.

The voice in his head said, "You have accomplished what you came to do. At worst, you would be captured and medically induced to spill the beans about what you had done. You do have a duty to conceal the knowledge you have. Your duty is to get out of here and back home."

And there was always the pill in the pharmaceutical pouch in his pocket. There were several good reasons why he should escape before security really tightened down after the full effect of the strike put the Republic on extra precautions. A weak, but positive reason to follow through with inviting her to go with him was that she could contribute her skills to their joint escape and they would look less suspicious than a man traveling alone.

He could see on the chalk board behind the ticket booth that the bus for Esfahan left in about forty five minutes. Decision time.

Against all logic and training, and in spite of the risks, he rose from his seat and went to the booth and bought a ticket to Esfahan. Now the die was cast. He had all the trip to decide not to go to Mitra and to escape on his own. Still, she pulled at him. He decided the risk was worth the reward. He would think about it on the bus, but as for now, he was going to Mitra.

Chapter 53

The old bus he boarded lumbered through the night, stopping only twice on its way to Esfahan. When he arrived in Esfahan in mid-morning, the city was teeming with activity. He took his duffel and walked a couple of blocks just to get away from the bus station. He was looking for a bath house where he could pay for a private shower and get cleaned up. He asked a merchant along the street and the merchant pointed north and said "Half a kilometer."

The price for a private shower was Twenty Five thousand Rials, about a dollar, which he paid in advance as required. The water was plenty hot and he luxuriated in the warmth after so many bruises and sprains. His hair was still matted with plaster dust and dirt from the blast and the collapse of the building he was hiding in. He even found dirt was caked in his eyebrows. It felt so good to be getting clean.

When he finished bathing, he put on the last of his clean clothes and his keffeiha and walked out into the scorching sunlight. He was thankful for his sunglasses as they not only reduced the discomfort of the glare, they afforded him some unrecognizability.

Using his compass and map, he set out toward the Ministry building where Mitra worked. He did not know if she would leave to get lunch or not, but he wanted to see her. It took more than an hour to walk to the building and he decided to wait outside the front door, but down the street a bit.

She did not show for lunch, so he decided to walk back down toward the restaurant where they had eaten earlier and duck into the lemon grove to find a place to sleep. When he got to the opening in the wall, there were no people in front of him or across the street from him, so he just walked into the opening without hesitation. He looped back to the inside of the wall and waited and watched for several minutes. No one came by. So, he found a mound of earth beneath a large lemon tree about fifty feet inside the opening and lay down using his duffel for a pillow. His position was well concealed by foliage and he relaxed enough to take a nap.

When he awakened, it was almost four. He stood carefully, looking around as he did. The grove was as deserted now as when he came in. He picked up his duffel and felt numerous sore spots in his body from the building collapse, but he ambled out of the opening in the wall and walked up the street toward the front door of the Ministry.

Chapter 54

(The following took place in French.)

"Ah, Monsieur Roman (pronouncing it Row Mahn, like a good French accent required.) You are awake. I am Doctor Ali Kasawneh. You are in the United States Army Doha Regional Hospital. You were brought here unconscious, by the air ambulance from Bushehr. We were told that you had been injured in a hotel that collapsed after an explosion in the road in front of the hotel you were staying at. Do you remember any of that?"

"Yes," said Lero, weakly. "I remember the explosion. Then everything came in on me."

"When you were brought in, we x-rayed you and fund you had broken bones in your lower right leg and you had two broken ribs. One of your ribs had punctured your left lung and we had to perform surgery on you. We put pins in your leg bones and it should heal alright in about six to eight weeks. Your lung is doing well now, after it re-inflated itself after the surgery. Your ribs will hurt you for six weeks or so. We conclude that you suffered a mild concussion, too. That will require medication and rest for a month or so. Other than that, you seem to be alright. Do you have any questions of me??

"Thank you, Dr. Kasawneh. I am very grateful. I guess I was banged up pretty much. I don't remember anything after the explosion until just now. Where is the lady that was traveling with me? Is she alright?"

"She is fine. She was exhausted after your surgery, so I gave her a sedative and she will probably sleep for six more hours. She is in a room down the hall. She may come and visit you when she awakes. Your employer, Mr. Murfree, called to say that we were to give you the best care possible and to call him the amount of the bill and he would cable the funds immediately. He must be very proud of you, Monsieur Roman."

"He is the best employer a man could have, Dr. Kasawneh," Lero sobbed.

"You get some rest now. We will check on you later to see if you feel like eating. We will take good care of you, Monsieur Roman."

"Thank you, Dr. Kasawneh," said Lero, with a grateful smile.

Chapter 55

Beri waited at the same place on the wall across the street and about a hundred yards from the front door of the Ministry building, like he had done before. A few minutes after four, people began to file out of the building. She came out in the main stream of people leaving. She looked up the block and saw him and turned to walk toward him. He saw her and met her part of the way. She was near the opening in the wall when they got near to each other. She led the way into the opening and curved around to wait for him behind the wall.

She said, "I am so surprised to see you. I thought you would be gone for a several days."

"I finished my assignment early and wanted to see you. I need to talk to you. Can we have dinner somewhere?"

She could not contain herself any longer. She grabbed onto his jacket and pulled herself up close to him and gave him a very thorough kiss.

"I am so glad you came. I am so glad to see you. I wondered if I would ever see you again," she said.

"Let's go to that restaurant with the nice booths and have dinner," he said.

"Sounds good," she said and took his arm with both of hers and cuddled against him.

They went back out of the opening in the wall and walked to the restaurant down in the next block.

She noticed that he walked a bit differently than before. She asked if he were okay.

He told her that there had been an accident and that he had gotten banged up a bit, but was much better now. No broken bones or stitches, but some substantial bruises.

"I would show you, but you would probably be revolted by my body," he said jokingly.

She looked at him directly and said, "I doubt that seriously."

Something pulled at him.

They only had to wait a moment at the restaurant before the waiter showed them to a booth. They slid in gratefully. The waiter handed him (naturally) a card with a handwritten menu of the day's offerings. He laid it down where she could see it and turned it around for her.

"Let's start with a platter of hummus and have the babaganoush," she suggested.

He said, "Fine with me. Two bottles of water, too."

"I would like some tea, too," she said.

After the waiter had taken their order, she looked at him for a time. He returned her look. Their minds were whirling, both thinking entirely different things, but both were anxious to hear what came next.

He took her hand in his and said, "Mitra, I am so drawn to you, but I need to tell you something before we go any farther."

"Oh, no," she said, taking in a deep breath and holding it. "You are married."

He blushed and guffawed.

"No, it is not that," he said.

"Mitra, this is such a leap for me. I want to tell you, but we have just met. My training tells me to be very wary, but my feelings tell me that I need to clear the air with you."

He paused while he gathered himself up to make his revelation.

"I am in the military. That is true. But, I am not a member of the Iranian military. I have been here on a surveillance mission and I am finished with my work here. I must leave before I am detected. I know this is sudden. I know that I am being foolish to even think that you would agree, but I want you to come with me. We can go to the west or wherever suits us. In time, you may grow indifferent to me and want your freedom. I will not hold you if you want to go. I just sense that we could have a sweet future together. I want to try to find that future with you somewhere where we could raise our children in safety and peace, somewhere where they can be free to follow their dreams. Isn't that a little bit crazy?"

She was stunned. She did not realize for a moment that her mouth had gaped open and she was staring at him. Then, she caught herself and snapped back to graceful composure.

"Oh, Beri. Oh, Beri, how difficult this has been for you. I am so glad you told me. I have had my suspicions that you were not the kind of Revolutionary Guard person we have encountered before. I am so glad to find that you are not one of them. Does anyone else here know?"

"No, you are the only person I have told," he said.

"What is your plan?" she asked.

"Traveling together gives each of us an advantage. I know how difficult it is for women to travel alone here. Having a woman with me will give me cover, too. They will be looking for a man alone. Please understand that I am not taking you with me for the cover. I will go alone if you must stay here. It is just a beneficial coincidence to my exit to have you with me. I know this requires a tremendous leap of faith for you, Mitra. You hardly know me, and now you know that I have deceived you from our first meeting. I know this has got to be nagging at you, telling you not to get mixed up any farther with this mysterious stranger."

"There are times when one must act on faith," she said. "The gentleness in you comes out right away, Beri. I know that you are not an evil person, much the opposite. You may someday ask me to leave, but I want to come with you to see what our future would be like together. I, too, know it is early, but little girls in this country are required to marry much older men without so much as an interview or first date. I would rather we had the time to get to know each other better first, but the situation requires faith."

She paused for a while, deep in thought, still looking at him across the table. The waiter brought their dinner.

She reached over and took his hand and looked earnestly into his eyes.

"Yes, I will go with you," she said. They looked at each other and smiled.

She studied him for a moment. Then, being the practical soul, she said, "But I have only the clothing on my back and the contents of my purse. What should we do?"

He reached into his jacket pocket and handed her a roll of bills.

"Here, now, you will not have to worry about money. You can buy whatever you need, including transportation. If we get separated, you can take care of yourself with that."

She let the bills unfold in her hand. Her eyes widened as she realized how much money he had handed her.

"I know it is early in our relationship, Mitra, but I feel drawn to you. If you come with me, you will have a time to consider if you want to continue it or break off and return. I know you may conclude that I am not such an interesting fellow after all and you may want to stay in the Republic. I will not try in any way to force you. You can tell the authorities that I kidnapped you to provide cover for me, if we get caught. You will be free to break off and return at any time, both as we leave and any time afterward. I want you to feel free and being free, I want you to want to decide on your own to stay with me."

"Oh, Beri, this is all so sudden. I understand, though. You must be on the way back in short order. I have dreamed of returning to the west for years. If I go with you, you must know that I make you the same bargain. If you tire of me, you need only say so and I will

301

leave you alone. I would be crushed, but we must have that understanding."

After she took a bite of hummus on a slice of pita bread, she asked: "How do you think it best to leave?" she asked.

"I think it best by sea," he said.

"Why don't we catch an overnight bus to Bushehr? We can rent a car there and drive down the coast. The coast highway approaches the shore quite closely about one hundred and fifty kilometers south of Bushehr."

"That sounds like a plan" he said and swiped a piece of pita through the hummus. He was lost in her green eyes.

Chapter 56

It was a bit past seven local time. General Haim was about to sit down with his wife for dinner. He reached for the remote to turn off the television during dinner and just as he got ready to push the button to do so, the screen flashed a brightly colored notice that there was breaking news. He delayed hitting the "Off" button long enough to listen to see if it were about anything interesting.

The announcer said: "We have just received a confirmed report that President Tartous has announced the death of the eighty year old Grand Ayatollah of the Islamic Republic of Iran.

His statement, read with obvious emotion, said that the Grand Ayatollah had died in his sleep in his personal quarters in Tehran. Efforts to awaken him this morning proved futile and his personal physician, Ali Akbar Abbas said that it appeared that the Grand Ayatollah suffered a nocturnal thrombosis, meaning that he had a heart attack in his sleep.

President Rafsanjani declared forty days of official mourning. He also said that all security forces would remain on full alert for the time being and that the Supreme Islamic Council would meet shortly to choose the next Grand Ayatollah. He said that a state funeral would take place tomorrow, as is Islamic custom. Many dignitaries who can reach Tehran from other countries are expected to attend.

Please stay tuned to Al Jazeera for information about further developments."

General Haim pushed the "Off" button and put down his newspaper and walked into the dining room for dinner.

www.ingramcontent.com/pod-product-compliance
Lightning Source LLC
Chambersburg PA
CBHW031251170626
46807CB00001B/97